'This changes things.'

'It does…?' she said, expectant. *What?*

He flicked her an impatient look. *'Obviously.* If we're not going to get a place together I suppose the logical alternative would be for me to move in with you.'

'Did I miss something? *Get a place together*…since when were we getting a place together?' Had he planned on mentioning this at some point? she wondered…

'Ah.' His speculative gaze skimmed her face. 'You were thinking of marriage…?'

Kim Lawrence lives on a farm in rural Anglesey. She runs two miles daily and finds this an excellent opportunity to unwind and seek inspiration for her writing! It also helps her keep up with her husband, two active sons, and the various stray animals which have adopted them. Always a fanatical consumer of fiction, she is now equally enthusiastic about writing. She loves a happy ending!

Recent titles by the same author:

LUCA'S SECRETARY BRIDE
THE SPANIARD'S LOVE-CHILD

HIS PREGNANCY BARGAIN

BY
KIM LAWRENCE

MILLS & BOON®

First published in Great Britain 2004
Paperback edition 2005
Harlequin Mills & Boon Limited,
Eton House, 18-24 Paradise Road, Richmond, Surrey TW9 1SR

© Kim Lawrence 2004

ISBN 0 263 84116 2

Set in Times Roman 10½ on 11¼ pt.
01-0105-53206

Printed and bound in Spain
by Litografia Rosés, S.A., Barcelona

CHAPTER ONE

'YOU said *what*?'

Even the anonymity of the phone could not disguise the natural authority in his most famous client's voice or, at that moment, the irritation and astonishment that had crept into the distinctive deep tones.

It had been a good idea *not* to have this particular conversation face to face, decided Malcolm, who was starting to feel uncomfortably like a man stuck between the proverbial rock and hard place. Yes, the analogy worked—if his sister was the rock, Luc could easily be considered a hard place.

Eyes slightly narrowed, Malcolm summoned an image of the younger man's startlingly good-looking face. The sharp jutting cheekbones, an aggressively angular jaw a wide, mobile mouth capable of issuing painfully blunt comments, and deep-set eyes. He gave a mental shudder as he considered those penetrating, spookily pale grey eyes. No doubt about it, Luc definitely constituted a hard place...a *very* hard place!

When Malcolm had initially met the first-time author of the sexy action thriller that had landed on his desk, he hadn't been able to believe his luck. Luc wasn't only incredibly photogenic, he was articulate and witty. Malcolm's visions of women snatching the book off the shelves after they'd seen his new client charming the pants off the public on the chat-show circuit were dashed when the guy had calmly announced that he was a writer, not a salesman.

Luc had spelt out his conditions to Malcolm. He wasn't available for interviews or photo opportunities; in fact he wanted to remain anonymous. If the books weren't good enough to sell on their own merits, so be it.

Malcolm's argument that one unfortunate experience at the hands of the press was not sufficient reason to make a disastrous business decision had not impressed Luc who, never one to take anyone's word for anything, had had a clause inserted in his contract.

Malcolm injected a note of desperate *bonhomie* into his voice. 'I was sure you'd love to come for the weekend so I sort of, well, I...I said you would.'

Perversely the silence that greeted his confession was more nerve-shredding than a tirade of angry abuse might be—Luc didn't get loud when he was mad.

The words 'soft but deadly' sprang unbidden into Malcolm's head.

'It'll all be very casual. No need to dress up. Charming woman, my sister—everyone loves her parties.'

Luc squinted up at the wall he had just painted. It really hadn't looked that *blue* on the label and the room was north facing...too cold. It would have to go.

'Have you developed a sense of humour, Mal? Or have you gone totally insane?' The latter explanation seemed much more likely to Luc.

'I know how you get after you've delivered a book.'

'Relieved...?'

'A weekend in the country is just what you need,' pronounced the editor firmly.

'I live in the country,' came the deceptively gentle reminder.

'No, you live in the back of beyond,' Malcolm corrected with an audible shudder in his beautifully modulated voice. 'I'm talking about Sussex; they have pavements there.'

The observation made Luc smile, but Malcolm, on the other end of the line, didn't have the comfort of seeing the warmth it lent his lean, dark features.

'Only recently someone persuaded me that what I needed

was a place in town…losing touch with reality, someone said, I seem to recall…? Now who was that? Oh, I remember—*you*!'

'Good company, excellent food…' Malcolm had a rare talent for selective deafness, which came in handy at moments like this. 'You like old things, don't you…? My brother-in-law was a great collector and they tell me the house is Elizabethan in parts, a moat, the whole thing,' he finished vaguely before producing his winning argument. 'Ghosts…!'

'I beg your pardon?'

'They have a ghost—several, I expect. Never seen them myself, of course, but…people doing psychical research come to look in the cellar and they open to the public on bank holidays so it must be something special.'

At the other end of the line the thought of the landed gentry brought a disdainful sneer to Luc's face. Personal experience had not given him a rosy view of the families who had once divided the wealth of the country between them. His father had worked on an estate as a forester until the titled owners had decided to turf him out of his tied cottage.

A job and home lost in one fell swoop, and all his dad had done was tug his forelock respectfully when they had explained that tourists were a more cost-effective way to utilise their resources. It was the meekness, the way he had accepted his fate that had filled Luc, then ten, with seething anger.

He had resolved on the spot that he would never bow and scrape to anyone. This resolve had been hardened into grim resolution as he had watched the defeated droop of his father's shoulders become permanent over the months that had followed.

He had been more adaptable than his father, who had struggled to fit in the large industrial town they had moved to. It hadn't been an accident that he'd lost the country burr that had made him the obvious target of bullies in the inner-city school.

Luc was a survivor.

Malcolm continued. 'Gilbert left my sister pots of money. Do you shoot, Luc?'

'*Shoot?*' Luc ejaculated in a tone of disgust. 'What is this—*Gosford Park*?'

'I meant clays,' Malcolm hastened to explain amiably.

'The only thing I shoot are editors who accept invitations on my behalf.' A spasm of curiosity crossed his handsome face. 'I'm interested—you knew I wouldn't agree, so why on earth did you say I would?'

'I knew you wouldn't like it, but I just heard myself saying it.' Impossible of course to make someone like Luc understand. 'You don't know my sister,' Malcolm added darkly. 'When she wants something she's relentless, like a dripping tap.'

'Sounds like a delightful hostess,' Luc interjected drily.

'She's an enormous fan of yours. You'd be treated like royalty, I swear.'

'I have no desire to be treated as royalty and I would be a major disappointment as a house guest...'

'As a favour to me...?' his editor cajoled.

'She can have an autographed copy of my next book.'

'She already has one, your signature is really *very* easy to fake.'

Malcolm decided that Luc's reluctant laugh was a sign the younger man was mellowing and pressed his advantage.

'Laura's been on at me for ages about you. Now, with Megan being thirty next month, and the lawyer chap breaking his leg last minute...' A huge sigh reverberated down the line.

'Who or what is Megan?'

'My niece, lovely girl...not married.'

An expression of amused comprehension crossed Luc's lean face. 'Am I invited because your sister is looking for a mug to partner her daughter?'

'Megan is a lovely girl,' Malcolm protested. 'Great personality. Takes after her father in the looks department, of course, but you can't have everything.'

Luc listened in growing amusement to the flow of confidences...from the moment he had walked into Malcolm's office he had *wanted* to dislike the other man. He represented everything Luc despised, from his accent to his privileged background. Yet Malcolm also possessed charm, he was basically a very likeable guy and, as Luc had learnt, despite his vague attitude, no pushover when it came to business.

'Do all the members of your family live in a previous century?'

Malcolm Hall's voice took on an ill-used quality as he responded to this incredulous query. 'Well, really, Lucas, I don't think it's much to ask considering what I've done for you. You really can be selfish, do you know that?' he complained.

Luc didn't resent the observation; he considered it was essentially true. He didn't enjoy money for its own sake, but he did enjoy the freedom it gave him. He considered himself a lucky man that doing what he enjoyed enabled him to live life on his terms.

It hadn't felt like it at the time, but with hindsight Luc recognised that losing his business the way he had had been one of the best things that had happened to him. If it hadn't been for his embezzling ex-partner he would never have shut himself in a room and worked for three weeks solid on the novel he had always *meant* to finish.

'I suppose I could tell Laura you have flu...'

'You can tell *Laura* anything you like, so long as it isn't I'd love to come to her party.' He liked Malcolm but that didn't mean he had the slightest intention of enduring a weekend being nice to people he had nothing whatever in common with.

It hadn't required enormous powers of deduction to discover where he lived, just a sneaky look in her uncle's address book.

Lucas Patrick, the best-selling author of a string of commercial and critically acclaimed novels, resided in the penthouse apartment of a warehouse conversion beside the river, the one that had won a whole bunch of awards the previous year. It was an address that didn't appear on the flyleaf of his numerous novels, but then neither did a suitably moody-looking black-and-white snapshot of the author.

Was the man genuinely allergic to publicity or was it a clever marketing ploy? Megan was not sure, but what was indisputable was that his point-blank refusal to promote his books had boosted his sales and turned him into an enigmatic hero-type figure not unlike the one that featured in his books. And Uncle Malcolm had been no help; the only thing he had let slip was that his most famous client was single and young.

If, when he went public, the writer turned out in the end to have middle-aged spread or a receding hairline there were going to be a lot of disappointed fans out there, her own mother included! she thought with a wry smile. Megan hoped he was presentable—it would make her idea a lot easier to pull off.

She paused, her finger hovering above the appropriate button, seized by last minute doubts about what she was doing. Last night this had seemed a truly inspired idea. In the cold light of day she didn't feel quite so confident that she was doing the right thing…she was even starting to wonder if it might not be a little crazy…?

But then desperate circumstances, she reminded herself, called for desperate measures!

What was the worst that could happen…?

Nothing as bad as what was going to happen if she didn't take some drastic action. Last Easter's efforts were still indelibly etched in Megan's mind. It had been totally excruciating and obvious to everybody but the hostess herself that the investment banker she had invited for the weekend as a potential husband for her spinster daughter was gay.

Megan loved her mother dearly, in fact she would have been the perfect parent if it weren't for her unswerving devotion to marrying off Megan!

Laura Semple had a simple philosophy—no woman could be happy without a man.

The conversation they had had over breakfast that very morning was more or less the same one they'd been having ever since Megan had decided not to marry the ever-so-suitable Brian four years earlier. Brian, who had turned out to be, not caring and protective in a charming, old-fashioned way, but a fully-fledged, possessive control freak who wanted her to account for every minute of her day and who got jealous when she talked to another man—*any* man.

Megan considered herself to have had a lucky escape, a view not shared by her mother.

'Of course I'm proud of what you've achieved, darling, but you can't tell me you're happy…not *really* happy.'

'*You* don't have a man, Mum.'

'That,' Laura rebutted firmly, 'is not the same thing at all. I'll never love a man the way I did your father.'

Megan saw the tears in her mother's eyes before she turned her head.

'There are lots of different loves.' Her own throat thickened with emotion as she gently squeezed her mother's hand. 'And actually I am happy.'

Her claim met with polite but open scepticism.

'I *promise* you, Mum, I'm perfectly content.'

'"Content" is a very middle-aged word, Megan,' her mother disapproved with a sigh.

'Maybe I'm one of those people that are born middle-aged…?'

'Oh, I know you put a brave face on it,' Laura continued, ignoring this flippant interjection. 'But, no matter what they say, no woman is totally fulfilled without a man.'

Megan bit her tongue and carried on smiling, past experience had taught her it was a waste of breath to argue this particular point.

'In your case a strong man I think,' Laura mused. 'One who isn't intimidated by your brains. Now *Lucas Patrick* doesn't sound to me like a man who is likely to lack confidence. The way he coped when his plane went down in the Andes…'

'That was his hero. He writes *fiction*, Mother,' Megan reminded her parent. 'He doesn't spend his life scaling impregnable peaks, busting international drug cartels or fighting off beautiful women who want to ravish him.'

'I am perfectly able to distinguish fact from fiction,' her mother retorted with dignity. 'But your uncle says he's scrupulous about his research and he *never* asks his hero to do anything he hasn't himself.'

'I seriously doubt if that includes crash-landing a plane and walking away without a scratch,' Megan muttered under her breath, then added in a louder voice, 'And the fact is you wouldn't know him from the man who delivers the milk. He'll probably turn out to be a regular anorak.' Her brow furrowed. 'And why on earth is he coming to one of your country weekends…?'

'I was a man short and your uncle Malcolm is his publisher; he's coming along with him. Well, he *was*—it turns out your uncle can't make it, but he says that Lucas is looking forward enormously to meeting us.'

'So you've only Uncle Malcolm's word that he's coming…?' In her experience, to stop his sister nagging her uncle would promise literally anything. 'Was Uncle Malcolm sober at the time…?'

'Don't be rude,' Laura reprimanded. 'And if you possess a skirt, pack it for the weekend, dear, do. You have very pretty legs—in fact you really are a very pretty girl, or would be if you took a little more effort. First impressions *do* count, Megan.'

Back to the task in hand, Megan squared her shoulders with resolution and, with a deep breath, she pressed the button. This idea might be a long shot but she just *had* to try. If Lucas Patrick was game she had figured out a fairly foolproof way to get her mother off her back *and* keep her happy.

A voice over the intercom responded almost immediately.

'About time too...' It was a deep voice, a bit gravelly at the edges and decidedly cranky which didn't bode too well for her plans.

'This is—'

'Yeah...yeah, you're here now. Just bring it up.' There was a buzz and the glass door swung open.

Megan shrugged and walked inside.

The lift rose smoothly and quickly, giving her no opportunity to change her mind. She knocked on the ajar door to the penthouse and heard the same impatient voice.

'Just bring it in—the money's on the table. If there are no extra anchovies don't take the tip.'

Oh, God, he's expecting a pizza and he's got a woman who wants him to pretend to be desperately in love with her!

Megan cleared her throat and looked curiously around the vast open-plan living space. With its steel support columns and lofty vaulted ceiling, it wasn't what she considered homey. She couldn't imagine coming here after a tough day, kicking off her shoes, pouring a glass of wine and switching on the telly. No, this was strictly bachelor territory and a rich bachelor at that, she thought, but then by all accounts the owner was worth a small fortune.

It was hard to gauge his taste as what furniture there was

was covered in dust-sheets. Her nose wrinkled; the place was permeated with the smell of paint and turps.

She cleared her throat and projected her voice to reach the invisible and grouchy presence. 'Mr Patrick, I'm afraid...' As the word left her mouth a lean, broad-shouldered figure materialised in a doorway.

Megan was pretty hopeless when it came to ages but she put this hunk somewhere in his early thirties. He was also tall, well over six feet, and dressed in tatty paint-stained jeans and a tee shirt that was clean but looked as though it had shrunk in the wash. The shrinkage meant it was impossible *not* to notice how well-developed his lean torso was. The tee shirt also revealed an inch or so of lean, flat belly and gave a glimpse of the thin line of dark hair that disappeared suggestively beneath the loose waistband of his jeans.

His dark flyaway brows drew together above a strong aquiline nose as he frowned suspiciously across at her.

'Who the hell are you?' he demanded as he dragged a hand through his collar-length sable hair that gleamed with health and was liberally speckled with blue paint. The jagged ends that rested on the nape of his brown neck suggested he hadn't seen the inside of a hair salon for some time.

This was the sort of guy who had women falling out of upper-storey windows to get a better look at him.

His presence undetected at first Luc had had an opportunity to study his intruder. Dressed casually as she was in jeans, there was nothing to distinguish this young woman from any number of others you saw in the street, except perhaps that this one appeared to carry herself with a certain air of quiet assurance.

She was tall and slim with hair like warm honey and candid china-blue eyes, which widened as they met his. The colour was so dramatically intense it could almost constitute an assault on the senses, he decided. The eyes had the sort of impact that made you not notice at first that her nose was undistinguished and her jaw slightly too determined. As far as he could tell she wasn't wearing any make-up, something she could get away with because her skin was smooth, the colour of milk and flawless.

Despite the fact she wasn't his type Luc felt his interest sharpen.

Megan's generous mouth tightened. Being a fairly direct person herself, she could appreciate the characteristic in others, but his question hadn't been brusque, more downright rude!

Clearly she had not made a favourable first impression on the decorator…she'd have to do a lot better with his employer if this wasn't going to be a total waste of time and energy.

'I'm Dr Semple.' Somehow what was meant to be a simple statement of fact emerged sounding pompous, but men this good-looking always made her feel slightly defensive… not that she had ever seen a man *this* good-looking.

His dark brows soared and the corners of his wide mouth twisted…something definitely cruel about that mouth, Megan decided, raising her glance hurriedly to eye level as something deep in her stomach twisted.

She sounded as cool and sure of herself as she looked. Luc liked her voice and found himself wondering what she would look like flustered. That hair spread out around her flushed… *Don't go there, Luc.*

He spread his expressive hands wide, inviting her inspection. 'Do I look like I have need of a doctor?' she heard him demand with vitality leaking out of every gorgeous pore.

He looked, from the top of his dark head to his… Her eyes dropped and her tummy did a crazy little back flip as she registered that his feet were the same even, toasty brown as the rest of him—at least the bits she could see. Not that she had any desire to see any more—what she was seeing was quite enough!

No doubt he'd be standing there oozing the same level of self-assurance if he had been bare all over.

Megan lowered her eyes quickly as the image that accompanied this maverick thought brought a lick of heat to her pale cheeks.

'I'm not that sort of doctor,' she mumbled. With thoughts like hers it was just as well—she'd have been struck off!

When she looked up a moment later he was still surveying her in unfriendly silence. The moment and the silence lasted too long for her comfort. His expression remained vaguely hostile as he brushed a hand carelessly along his chiselled jaw—God, but this man had perfect bones!—leaving a faint smudge of paint against his olive skin.

For no logical reason she could figure, she found herself wondering what he would do if she licked her finger and wiped the offending mark away from his smooth, blemish-free skin. She took a deep breath, horrified by the direction of her wilful imagination.

It was time to take control here.

CHAPTER TWO

Luc had obviously reached the same conclusion and he got in before Megan.

'I don't know how you got in here, *Doctor*, but I'd like you to go back the way you came.'

Or else—unspoken but definite, the warning hung in the air.

It wasn't his threatening posture that bothered Megan, it was the illicit and inexplicable little shiver that traced a path up her spine. Good looks, even ones as spectacular as his, she could take in her stride. At a subconscious level she recognised it was the earthy, sensual quality that he possessed in abundance that had her standing there like some inarticulate teenager.

She blinked, determined to rectify any false impression she had given that she was a brainless bimbo. Actually she had forgotten to breathe, which might account for the dizzy sensation; she took a deep, gulping gasp and immediately felt a little better.

'Well, unless your short-term memory is shot to hell you ought to know…you asked me in,' she reminded him.

A flicker of something that might have been surprise flickered behind his sensational eyes for a split second before shoulders that any athlete would have envied lifted fractionally. 'And now I'm asking you to leave.'

This was no invitation—it was an order.

Megan's chin went up the same way it had been doing, if her mother was to be believed, for twenty-nine years whenever she had been told what to do. 'I came to see Mr Patrick.'

The grey eyes narrowed but stayed like lasers on her focused face. The dark rings surrounding his irises highlighted the pale metallic colour of his eyes.

Did he ever blink…?

He gave another graceful shrug. 'Well, as you can see, I'm the only one here.' He placed the towel he had been holding on a dust-cloth covered table and picked up a bottle of mineral water. He unscrewed the top and raised it to his lips.

So she'd been dismissed…? Did he actually think she was going to leave just because he told her to…? The angry glow in her eyes became distracted as she watched the contraction of muscles in his brown neck as he swallowed, there was a faint sheen of moisture on his skin. She looked away.

'Is Mr Patrick likely to be home soon?'

'Are you a friend of his or just a groupie?'

Her outraged attention swung back to his mocking, handsome face. His insulting cynicism brought an angry flush to her face, or did that rise in temperature have something to do with the beads of moisture he brushed off his sensual lips…?

'I hardly think that's any of your business,' she retorted haughtily. 'Perhaps you'd like to carry on with whatever Mr Patrick is paying you to do, other than eat pizzas.'

He looked amused. 'Even a humble painter is allowed a lunch break, *Doctor*. Would you like me to give the boss a message?' he offered, casually looping the towel around his neck. The action revealed another inch of smooth, hard flesh.

Megan swallowed and lowered her gaze. 'It's personal.'

'You wish.'

Pale grey eyes clashed with turbulent blue.

'I'll wait,' she announced frigidly. Other than physically remove her, he couldn't do much about it, and if he did come over heavy handed she'd stick him with a lawsuit for assault before he could blink!

'Suit yourself,' he drawled. 'But then I'm sure you generally do.' This woman had spoilt and privileged written all over her, from her smooth voice to her assured manner.

Just as Megan's bottom made contact with the dust-sheet-covered chair there was a sudden upheaval beneath her that sent her with a startled shriek to her feet.

A bundle of spitting fury struck out at her with sharp claws as it hurtled across the room like a ginger flash of lightning.

'Ouch!' she yelled. 'That thing scratched me.' Rolling up the right leg of her jeans revealed a long, though admittedly shallow, scratch along her calf.

'That thing is called Sybil and you did sit on her. Poor cat,' he crooned to the cat from the flat downstairs.

Megan wasn't surprised to see the animal respond to his velvety croon, and in lightning transformation. *That voice...!* She could imagine any number of women who were old enough to know better purring if he used that voice on them.

'Is the skin broken?'

'I'll live,' she replied, rolling down her trouser leg. Superficial or not, the scratch stung. 'Do you have any idea when he'll be back?'

'Who?'

Megan gave an impatient grimace. 'Mr Patrick.'

'Oh, him...he'll be back in the country some time next month, I understand.'

Megan, her high hopes dashed by the casual revelation, felt her face fall. 'But he has to be back before then,' she protested.

'Really...?'

'He's spending next weekend in the country with us.'

'Maybe it slipped his mind...?'

Megan, who had flopped disconsolately into the cat-free chair, cast him a look of scorn. 'Or maybe Uncle Malcolm lied through his teeth,' she muttered half to herself.

Look on the bright side, she told herself, no eligible suitor equalled not being paired off with anyone, and it always had been a long shot.

The bad news was there would be other weekends!

'Malcolm Hall is your uncle?'

Megan shot him a startled glance and began to sneeze. 'You know him?' She felt another sneeze building and began to ransack her bag for tissues, she found the packet just in time.

'We're not members of the same club,' she heard him drawling scornfully when her sneezes subsided. 'And I don't play golf…but they let us unskilled labourers into quite a few places these days.'

Megan gave her pink nose a last angry scrub, her china-blue eyes snapping with anger. Where did this man get off automatically assuming she was some sort of snob? There was only one person here guilty of judging by appearances and it wasn't Megan!

'In my book decorators aren't unskilled, although…' she allowed her gaze to travel significantly over his paint-stained person '…in your case…'

'I'm helping out a friend.'

'So what is your actual day job?'

'I do a bit of this, a bit of that,' he revealed casually.'

'You don't have a regular job?' Megan's voice lifted in amazement—like most of her friends, her life revolved around the demands of work.

Luc found the fact she was looking at him as though he were a rare specimen amusing. 'I don't starve and I don't sponge.'

Megan was immediately embarrassed. 'I never imagined that you…it really isn't any of my business how you live your life, Mr…'

'Not being tied down to a nine-to-five routine gives me time to write. Some of my work is even now sitting on your uncle's desk.'

'You want to be a writer?' That would explain his instant

recognition of her uncle's name. Though he had to be incredibly naive if he thought the work of every unknown who sent in an unsolicited manuscript ended up on her uncle's desk. You had to produce something very special indeed to get that far.

Much more likely his work was languishing at the bottom of a pile on some junior's desk. Being a naturally kind person, Megan didn't have the heart to explain the brutal facts of the publishing business to him.

'Is there any reason why I shouldn't be a writer?'

Her eyes swept over his tall, impressive figure. The truth was he exuded so much vitality and energy Megan couldn't imagine him doing anything that required long periods of physical immobility.

Megan smiled sunnily and had the satisfaction of hearing his teeth grate. 'Listen, I don't know the first thing about publishing and I have no influence with my uncle but if you're serious about writing I think it would probably be a good idea to find yourself an agent.'

'Anybody you could recommend…?'

'Afraid not.'

'Maybe you should see a doctor,' he observed with a grimace as she began to sneeze loudly again.

'Look, I'm not in publishing, but good luck and don't worry—' Megan sniffed '—I'm not ill. I'm allergic to cats,' she explained as she got to her feet.

'Now, if you'll excuse me…?' She nodded, and slung the soft leather satchel she carried over her shoulder and smoothed down her jacket.

The long, lean, intensely aggravating stranger didn't step aside to let her pass. Instead he tilted his head back slightly to look curiously down at her and asked, 'What kind of doctor are you?'

'I'm a research chemist.'

'Interesting,' he said, looking and sounding as though he meant it.

'It has its moments.' Her bag hit her thigh as she hitched it on her shoulder and she winced as the fabric of her jeans rubbed against the fresh scratches on her leg.

'You should put some antiseptic on that; cat scratches can get infected. If you like I've got some…'

An image of those long brown fingers moving over her skin flashed into Megan's head. The reaction to the image was immediate and intense; the surface of her skin broke out in a rash of goose-bumps; her skin tingled; her sensitive stomach muscles contracted violently.

Her wide eyes lifted and collided with a steel-grey interrogative stare. There was a silence. The electric tension in the air had to be a product of her imagination, but it felt disturbingly real.

'That won't be necessary,' she replied huskily. 'But thanks for the offer.'

Adopting a brisk, decisive air, she stepped forward. She caught her lower lip between her teeth and hesitated when he didn't move. There was room to edge past, but that would mean touching him. The desire to get away from this man's disturbing presence was strong, but her reluctance to make physical contact was stronger. 'I'm sorry to have held you up…'

'So Lucas Patrick is a friend of yours…?'

'Actually I've never met the man in my life,' she admitted. 'Now if—'

'You're a fan, then?' he theorised, talking across her. 'If you leave your address, perhaps he'll send you an autograph.'

'Do I look stupid enough to give a total stranger my address?' she demanded.'

The dark, satanically slanted brows lifted, but Megan had no more intention of responding to the gesture than she did the quivery demands of her oversensitive tummy muscles.

'And I don't want his damned autograph,' she grunted, blushing darkly.

'Then you don't like his books?'

'I've read some of his earlier ones, I can see why he's popular,' she observed diplomatically.

'But not with you?' he suggested shrewdly.

'I think he's slightly overrated.' Unfairly she vented her antagonism towards this man on the absent and talented author.

She expelled a silent breath of relief as he finally moved aside to let her pass. As she did so she lifted her head as a thought occurred to her. 'Have you actually *met* Lucas Patrick?'

'In passing.'

Megan's eyes widened. He didn't seem to appreciate this put him in a pretty unique category. 'Really—! And how did he seem?'

'Seem?'

'What was he like?'

'He seemed a pretty ordinary sort of guy to me,' he divulged disappointingly.

'Then is he…what does he look like?' She shook her head. 'No, on second thoughts, don't tell me, leave me with my illusions—though if you happened to nod when I said balding, or paunchy, that wouldn't be totally out of order, would it?'

'I thought your uncle was his editor?'

'He is, but Uncle Malcolm's lips are sealed when it comes to Lucas Patrick,' she admitted regretfully.

'And you're curious…?'

A grin of pure mischief spread across Megan's face. 'A girl always likes to know ahead of time what her future husband looks like.'

'Future *husband*…?'

The look of horror etched on his dark, dramatically perfect face could not have been more heartfelt had she just announced her intention to marry him. Megan loosed a gurgle of laughter. 'A joke,' she placated.

'He might not think so,' the tall stranger observed as he scanned her amused face.

'Then he has no sense of humour,' Megan proclaimed.

'You still haven't said what brought you here…'

Halfway to the door, Megan turned back at the sound of his voice. Why not? the reckless voice in her head suggested. You're never going to see the man again. Maybe there was something in that old maxim that it was easier to discuss things with a stranger.

'My mother wants me to be happy.' She began to experience a familiar tightness in her chest and she sat down cautiously on the arm of a chair.

'And that's a problem?' Luc watched her fumble in her bag.

'She believes no woman is complete without a man.'

'And you don't have one.'

Megan's chin went up. 'I don't *want* one,' she rebutted firmly. Her fingers closed over the inhaler she never went out without and she gave a sigh of relief. 'At regular intervals she tries to set me up with someone she imagines…'

'Is good breeding stock…' came the straight-faced suggestion.

Megan's eyes narrowed. 'Will make me happy,' she corrected and raised the inhaler to her mouth. The relief was almost immediate. 'This is why I avoid cats,' she said, anticipating his question.

'You have asthma?' he queried, watching the rapid rise and fall of her chest.

'A little,' she admitted. She went to rise but a large hand fell on her shoulder, anchoring her to the spot. Her eyes slid from his brown fingers to his face.

'Take a minute to get your breath,' he suggested, actually it was more than a suggestion, it was a quiet command.

Normally Megan didn't respond well to commands but on this occasion she found herself strangely willing to let it pass. His concern, even though unnecessary was oddly comforting.

'Can I get you anything? A glass of water?'

She nodded; her throat felt oddly achy and constricted.

Without a further comment he left and returned with a glass of water. He stood there, arms folded across his chest while she drank. Megan was very conscious of his silent presence. He wasn't the sort of man you could forget was there.

'Thank you,' she said politely, handing back the empty glass. Their fingers touched briefly during the exchange; the contact did uncomfortable things to Megan's pulse.

'Can I call anyone for you?'

'Gracious, no!' Very conscious of her warm cheeks, she forced a smile but didn't meet his eyes. 'I'm fine.'

'Despite a matchmaking mother.'

The comment brought her head up. 'I've tried everything to put her off,' she admitted ruefully. 'Nothing works.'

Head tilted a little to one side, a frown deepening the line between his flyaway brows, he scanned her face. 'What are you…thirty…?'

The almost-spot-on estimate disconcerted her; she had enough female vanity to feel peeved.

'Sorry, have I touched a nerve?'

Megan glared at him. 'No, you haven't,' she denied angrily. 'I have no problem with being thirty…actually, *almost* thirty.'

'Good for you,' he interposed with silken gravity. 'Don't you think at *almost* thirty it's time you told your mother to mind her own business?'

Megan coloured angrily. He made it sound so simple, but then it probably was, if you had no problem trampling all over the feelings of people you loved. 'Oh, why didn't I think of that? Of course, it might be because I don't want to hurt my mother.'

His shoulders lifted in a disdainful shrug. 'Well, if you don't mind people running your life…?'

'My mother doesn't run my life!' she flared.

'No?'

Megan clenched her teeth. 'No, she doesn't. She has had a tough time the last few years,' she informed him, swallowing past the emotional lump in her throat. 'She isn't some cold control freak, she is just a caring mum who wants to see her daughter happy and settled.' She dragged a frustrated hand through her hair and gave a dejected sigh. 'Unfortunately happy and settled for her equates with a man and marriage, which is why I had this idea…a sort of line-of-least-resistance thing.'

Luc watched as she gazed abstractedly into the distance, her smooth brow furrowed.

'Least resistance…?' he probed softly.

She nodded. 'If I could get one of the prospective grooms to pretend to be smitten, Mum would be happy and leave me to get on with more important things.'

Luc's deep-set eyes widened slightly as comprehension struck home. 'And what do you consider important?'

'My job.'

'You can't live and breathe your job.'

'My work is very demanding; it leaves no time for relationships. '

'So you're married to your career.'

She frowned; he made her sound freaky. 'I've nothing against marriage, but I don't think I'll ever find a man who is willing to take what little I would have to give.'

'You don't have a very high opinion of men.'

'I'm a pragmatist.'

'You think you were being pragmatic when you came here to ask Lucas Patrick to…*pretend to be smitten…*?'

A mortified flush mounted Megan's cheeks—when he said it, it sounded even more off the wall. 'I didn't say that.'

'But that's what you came here for?'

'It's not as crazy as it sounds.'

'Did I say it was crazy? I'm just wondering…what was going to be in it for him?'

CHAPTER THREE

MEGAN frowned. *'In it…?'*

'As in what would he get out of it?' Luc looked into her bewildered face and laughed. 'You thought he'd do it out of the goodness of his heart.' His mobile lips lifted cynically at the corners. 'You really never have met Lucas Patrick, have you?'

'And unlike you I'd prefer not to bad-mouth him in his absence.'

For some reason her angry reproach caused him to laugh. It was a deep, warm, uninhibited sound that made Megan's pulse rate quicken. 'Just bad-mouth his books…?'

She wrenched her appreciative stare from the mesh of fine lines around his smiling grey eyes and frowned. 'Don't put words in my mouth,' she warned him.

The stern warning brought Luc's attention to her lips; she was attempting to compress them into a thin, disapproving line. As he contemplated the soft, cushiony contours it took considerable self-discipline to prevent his thoughts diverting into a carnal direction.

'And I'm sure Mr Patrick has survived worse than anything I might say about him. And actually,' she added, 'I happen to think that he's quite a talented writer.'

'But you were willing to overlook his dubious literary talent in the interests of a quiet life?' he questioned.

The soft charge brought a guilty flush to her cheeks. She squared her shoulders and sighed. 'All right, I admit it was a pretty daft idea, but as the man isn't here it's fairly academic, isn't it?'

'Maybe…'

'There's no *maybe* about it,' she rebutted morosely.

'Would I be right in assuming that nobody at this house party, including your mother, has ever met Lucas Patrick…?'

'Well, no, since Uncle Mal won't be coming I don't suppose…but I don't see what that has to do with anything, Mr…what is your name anyhow?' The weirdness of discussing such personal things with a total stranger whose name she didn't even know suddenly struck Megan forcibly.

A slow, wolfish grin split the nameless stranger's lean, dark face, revealing a set of white even teeth and causing her stomach to flip. Not only had she lost all control over what came out of her mouth, she had lost control of her nervous system as well!

'To cut down on confusion, perhaps it's better if you just call me Lucas…?' he suggested smoothly.

'*What*…?' Megan's impatient expression vanished as her eyes snapped open to their fullest extent. God, he couldn't be saying what she thought he was…*could he*…?

She scanned his face with suspicion. 'What are you suggesting?'

'I'm suggesting that you need a face to fit your fantasy lover.' He adopted an expression of enquiry. 'Is there anything wrong with this one?' His fluid gesture indicated his own lean face.

Megan looked at the golden toned skin stretched across the perfect arrangement of strong angles and intriguing hollows and went perfectly pale.

'You're insane.' Despite her attitude of total conviction, there was a small voice in her head that said it could just work…

'I'm assuming you weren't expecting Lucas Patrick to actually marry you…?'

'Don't be absurd,' she breathed faintly. Like a hypnotised rabbit, she couldn't take her eyes off his face. That voice in her head was getting louder.

'Did you have a time factor in mind…?' When she

looked back at him blankly he spelt it out. 'How long did you imagine this fake romance had to last? Six months or so?'

'I hadn't really thought that far ahead.'

His disturbing eyes glittering from beneath the sweep of long, curling ebony lashes, he slanted her a sardonic look.

'Oh, I guess so,' she conceded crossly. 'If you're suggesting anyone is going to believe you're a famous author...' She gave a forced laugh.

'Nobody has the faintest idea what Lucas Patrick looks like.'

'They may not know what he looks like—' she deliberately trailed her eyes along the long, lean lines of his athletic frame; about midway she lost her scornful air '—but I think they might know what he *doesn't* look like,' she finished hoarsely.

His self-satisfied air intensified as he surveyed her heated cheeks. 'If I had claimed to be him when you walked in you'd have been none the wiser.'

'Nonsense! Of course I would,' she instantly rebutted indignantly. 'What do you take me for?'

A look she couldn't quite decipher flickered at the back of his steely, dark-lashed eyes. 'Someone who thinks they can tell, just by looking at a person, who he is...or should I say what he does? The two seem to be the same thing as far as you're concerned.'

'Of course I can't.'

'And neither can anyone else. The fact is you assumed I was the hired help because of the way I'm dressed. If I came out of the bedroom with a stethoscope around my neck you'd have assumed I was a doctor. It's all about props.'

'This is all academic...I'm not going to invite a total stranger into my home.'

'Afraid I'll steal the silver?'

She shook her head and refused to respond to this taunt. 'This isn't going to happen. Even if you did carry it off...'

'I will,' he promised.

His smug smile made her frown. 'Even if you did my mother is never going to believe I'm attracted to you.' Then she would be wrong wouldn't she?

'What's wrong with me?'

'You're simply not my type.'

'What is your type?'

'Shall we drop this subject?'

'Because you find it uncomfortable?' The idea seemed to amuse him.

'I find *you* uncomfortable.' Too much information, Megan, she told herself not liking the thoughtful expression on his face. Recalling his earlier cynical comments, she asked, 'What do *you* get out of it?'

He smiled. 'Your uncle Malcolm looks at my manuscript.'

So that was it. 'If you've written a load of rubbish, nothing I say is going to make Uncle Malcolm publish you.'

'It isn't rubbish; it's good.'

'You're very confident.'

He didn't deny her accusation. 'I just need a break and you need a lover.'

'A *fake* lover.'

'I'm applying for the job...?'

Megan clutched her head and groaned. 'I must be mad!'

'You won't regret this,' he promised, extending his hand.

Megan, who was pretty sure she would regret it, allowed her fingers to be enclosed in his firm grip. A shot of heat zapped through her body.

She was regretting it already. She carried on regretting it and questioning her sanity during the next twenty-four hours. In the end it didn't matter.

Her fake lover was a no-show.

CHAPTER FOUR

THE day was grey and drizzly, there had been no buyers for a brisk walk, so Megan hadn't had company when she'd walked the dogs. She was still in her muddy shoes and outdoor clothes when a noisy Land Rover drew up onto the gravelled forecourt right beside a Porsche and a Mercedes. She stopped towelling the muddy terrier and got to her feet, her heart pounding—*please let it not be him...!*

'I wonder who that is?' her mother asked with a frown. 'I do wish you'd fetch the dogs in through the kitchen when we've got guests,' she remonstrated gently. 'Hilary will have hysterics if they go within ten yards of her...tiresome woman,' she added to herself. 'Down, Fred,' she added sternly to the large dog who had planted his damp paws on her stomach.

'I can't imagine who it is,' Megan replied, her heart thumping madly in her chest.

Her mother looked at her sharply. 'Are you feeling all right, Megan?' She considered her daughter's face with a frown. 'You look a little flushed.'

'Me? I'm fine, absolutely fine!' The cheerful smile she pinned on her face felt as though it was about to crack...or was that her face? 'I'll go and see who it is, shall I?' she added brightly.

'Would you, dear?'

Megan was already running across towards the vehicle, her boots crunching on the gravel. Seconds later she arrived breathless and quivering with tension.

'You're late!' she fired as the tall figure stepped with lithe, fluid ease from the disreputable-looking four-wheel drive. 'I thought you weren't coming.' If she was honest

she had been relieved when she had thought he wasn't hon-
ouring their bargain.

'Something came up,' he revealed casually.

'And it didn't occur to you to let me know,' she quivered
accusingly.

One dark brow angled sardonically. 'Don't you think you
should wait until we are irresistibly attracted before you get
possessive…?' he suggested mildly.

The sarcasm brought an angry sparkle to her eyes. 'This
might be a joke to you, but—'

'Not a joke,' he interposed. 'But I don't see any reason
we can't make the best of it. We might even enjoy our-
selves…'

'*Enjoy?* Are you insane?' Then, transferring her attention
to the off-roader, she continued without missing a beat. 'Is
that yours?'

If I had an ounce of foresight, she thought, I would have
considered the question of transport and hired him the sort
of car people would expect a best-selling author to drive
around in. If I had any foresight I wouldn't have done this
at all.

'No, I stole it on the way here,' he returned, straight-
faced. His dark eyes moved from the tendrils of hair that
curled damply around her fair skinned face to her wide,
anxious eyes. 'Is that a problem?'

Megan tore her attention from the Land Rover and cast
him a look of seething dislike…as she did so she immediately realised that nobody would notice if he rolled up riding
a child's tricycle!

'Oh, my God…' she groaned, grabbing agitated handfuls
of damp hair. '*Look at you!*'

She followed her own instructions and allowed her glance
to travel down the long, lean length of him once more. It
was a cue for a heat flash to consume her all over again.

He was sheathed from head to toe in black. The leather,
age-softened jacket he wore was moulded to truly fantastic

shoulders. It hung open to reveal a plain white tee shirt that clung to his powerful chest and lean, washboard belly. His dark moleskins followed the muscular contours of long, powerful thighs. God, was that a hole in the knee…? She despaired that a tiny glimpse of flesh could make her break out in a sweat.

This was never going to work.

'What's wrong with me?'

Nothing, if you liked being hit over the head with sex appeal.

'Everything!' she snapped in a doom-laden drone.

His mobile mouth quirked at the corners; he didn't appear particularly chastened by her pronouncement. 'Harsh.'

'You might have made an effort to look less…' *Sexy.* Her eyes slid from his as she added huskily, 'More…like a writer. And you could have shaved; you look like you haven't been to bed.'

He lifted a hand to the strong curve of his jaw covered with a layer of dark stubble and grinned. 'I haven't.' He had had an idea for his next book; when inspiration struck, he listened. He had worked through the night to get it down on paper.

'Spare me the details of your conquests,' she begged.

'Relax, nobody knows what this particular writer looks like.' Persuasive as his argument was, it didn't stop her feeling as though she had made a terrible mistake. 'And isn't this the way they want your writer to look…?'

'Want? That's the problem—nobody actually really *believes* he looks like a Byronic hero. You look too good to be true—they'll smell a rat.' But he wasn't true, was he? He was a fake. He was also quite simply the most impossibly good-looking male she had ever seen.

'Why, thank you.'

'Look, if you're not going to take this seriously drive away now,' she instructed. This was almost certainly going to go wrong. 'No,' she added urgently. 'Drive away anyway. This was a very bad idea.'

'Chill out,' he drawled, looking infuriatingly laid-back.

The suggestion made her see red. 'Chill out? *Chill out!*' she repeated in a shrill squeak. 'Easy for you to say. If this goes wrong people aren't going to think you're the desperate sort of woman who has to resort to hire a lover!' she declared with a groan of self-recrimination.

He scanned her anguished face, with deep-set eyes that revealed none of his feelings. 'Presumably they'll just think I'm a gigolo,' he cut back. 'Actually I wasn't aware that sleeping with you was part of the deal, but what the hell?' His sensual mouth formed a wide smile that didn't touch his eyes. 'I'll throw that in for free.'

There was a lengthy silence while Megan cleared her head of disturbing images and sounds: A darkened room, soft groans, intimate murmurs, two sweat-soaked bodies intimately entwined…. She tugged fretfully at the neck of her sweater as she fought for breath. Inch by inch she fought her way back to control…or something that passed for it.

'God, don't go sensitive on me,' she begged, still haunted by the humiliating memory of the suffocating white-hot excitement she had felt when she had imagined— She caught her breath sharply. Don't go there, Megan, she told herself sternly.

'You know I wasn't speaking literally,' she contended calmly, meeting his eyes. 'I've simply realised I can't go through with it. Late in the day, I know, but don't worry— I'll still have a word with Uncle Malcolm. He'll look at your manuscript, I promise.'

Megan heard the crunch of gravel behind her and looked over her shoulder. Her mother was advancing towards them. When her attention flickered back to her co-conspirator he was shaking his head.

'I don't want charity. I'm perfectly prepared to fulfil my side of the bargain.'

Megan looked at him with frustrated incomprehension.

His body curved towards her. 'Smile, sweetheart, and try and remember you've just found the man of your dreams.'

'Nightmares, more like.'

He laughed and touched her cheek with the back of his hand. It was so light it barely constituted a brush but Megan experienced an electrical thrill that travelled all the way to her toes. She stepped backwards, her nostrils flared as she tried not to breathe in the warm male fragrance that made her stomach flip. 'Well, I suppose we'll just have to make the best of it.'

'Is this a friend of yours, Megan?'

Megan, her hands held up in front of her, backed farther away from the tall, handsome figure who was the object of her mother's obvious appreciation.

'No—whatever gave you that idea?' The sharpness of her tone brought her mother's frowning attention to her own face. 'I've never seen him before in my life.'

He spared her a sideways look of amusement as he advanced towards her mother with his hand outstretched. 'You can know some people for years and never really know them, others you can know seconds and there's a rapport—' He broke off and gave a self-conscious laugh. 'Does that sound crazy?'

Megan was staggered to see her mother looking as though he'd just said something profound instead of something profoundly silly.

'Not at all, I know *exactly* what you mean!' Laura exclaimed.

'I think it's dangerous to go on first impressions,' Megan inserted drily.

'You're not a romantic?'

'My daughter is a cynic, Mr...'

'I'm Lucas Patrick.'

Megan drew a deep breath and squared her slender shoulders. Well, that was it! With those words he had committed them both for better or worse…she suspected the latter.

Laura took an audible deep breath and pressed her hand to her mouth. Megan felt a fresh spasm of guilt to see her mother's childlike delight.

'Of course you are.' She laughed. 'Why, this is marvellous.' A faint furrow appeared between her delicately arched brows. 'My brother told me you had flu…'

'Mal's prone to exaggeration, but then you'd know that.' Laura nodded happily. 'I had a head cold, that was all.' He looked around expectantly. 'Where is Mal?'

'Didn't he mention he couldn't make it?'

'No, that's a pity.'

Megan, who was amazed at how he had immersed himself in the part he was playing, watched with unwilling fascination as a troubled expression of suspicion spread across his handsome features.

'He did…you *were* expecting me…?' he pressed.

'Of course we were,' Laura the perfect hostess responded without skipping a beat. 'We just weren't sure when you'd be here, were we, darling?'

'No, we weren't.' Megan glanced at her watch, how many hours of this did she have to endure? The irony was this was a situation of her own making.

'So long as I'm not imposing.'

'Gracious, not at all. Actually we've been thrilled at the prospect of having you stay. Haven't we, darling?'

'Thrilled,' said Megan obediently.

'Megan has read all your books, haven't you?'

In full charm mode, his eyes crinkled delightfully at the corners, he turned his attention briefly to a squirming Megan. 'I think you've embarrassed…' he gave a quizzical look of apology '…Meg…?'

'Megan.'

The lack of animation in her response earned her a reproachful glare from her mother. God, he seemed to be enjoying himself…! If he wasn't a con man he'd missed his calling, she decided grimly. A man like that could convince a girl of almost anything, especially if she wanted to believe it! This was something worth keeping in mind the next time her hormones went haywire, she told herself.

'Megan will show you to your room, won't you, darling?'

'Thank you, Megan.'

'My pleasure,' she replied with equal insincerity.

'Please call me Luc,' he invited them.

'I have a French friend called, Luc,' Laura commented.

'My grandfather on my mother's side was French.'

'I knew there was something Gallic about you the moment I saw you…French men have such style,' Laura observed. 'Is your mother alive, Luc?'

'No, she died when I was nine. She named me after her own father, my grandfather.'

Behind her mother Megan shook her head and telegraphed a warning with her eyes. Her fake lover smiled back enigmatically.

'Do you speak French, Luc? I'll get someone to bring your luggage in…'

'No need, I travel light,' he said, extracting a rucksack from the back seat of the Land Rover.

'How refreshing,' Laura said, as though she were used to guests turning up carrying a rucksack that looked as if it was about to disintegrate. 'Show Luc up to the red room, Megan, then bring him down for tea… Then you can meet the other guests. Megan shot Lucas a questioning look.

'A quick shower and I'm all yours,' he promised.

Ignoring her mother's hissed instruction to, *for God's sake, smile, he's gorgeous*, she stalked towards the house with a face like thunder. She kept a tight-lipped silence until they reached the kitchen. Reaching the door that led to the back staircase, she turned and found that he was no longer at her shoulder but standing some yards away looking around the vast room.

'There really are an amazing number of original features intact,' he observed, opening the door of an original bread oven set in an alcove of the cavernous inglenook.

'Save it for my mother,' Megan, in no mood to discuss the architectural merits of her home, snapped. 'Did you have to lay it on with a trowel?' she demanded. 'Why on earth did you say you spoke French?'

'I didn't say I did.'

'You implied.'

'I do speak French.'

'Oh! And what was all that stuff about a French grand-father...?'

'My grandfather was French.'

Which was probably where he had inherited his dark Mediterranean colouring. 'You're not meant to be *you*, you're meant to be Lucas Patrick.'

'I am Lucas Patrick,' he contradicted.

Megan sighed. 'There's such a thing as overconfidence. Let's just hope the real Lucas Patrick isn't a litigious man.'

'You're an awful worrier, aren't you? Do you always assume the worst?'

'I only worry when there's something to worry about.' She scanned his dark face resentfully—he wasn't meant to be enjoying this. 'Aren't you even *slightly* nervous?'

'Not especially.'

'Well, you should be. From now on say as little as possible and follow my lead. Do you understand?' she asked him sternly. It was about time, she decided, to remind him just who was in control here. Her lips curved in a self-derisive smile; had she ever felt less in control in her life?

'Perhaps if you could write it down for me?'

'Very funny.' She sniffed. 'Come on, I suppose I'd better show you to your room. We'll take the back stairs.'

'Anyone would think you were ashamed of me,' he reproached.

Megan dished up a repressive glare but wasn't surprised

when he didn't look unduly subdued. 'There are six other people staying other than you. There's…'

When they reached the room her mother had allocated to him, she decided not to mention it was next to her own and that all the other guests were in a different wing entirely— she asked him to repeat the names of his fellow guests.

He ran his fingers across some carving in an ancient beam above the low doorway. 'Is this a test?'

'Were you actually listening to me?' she asked suspiciously.

'I was listening; your voice is like honey.'

Megan, her hand on the door handle, stilled. She was certain she had misheard what he had said. *'Pardon…?'*

'You have a beautiful voice. It flows…' His hands moved in an expressive fluid gesture before he sighed. 'I could listen to it all day…' Her voice was part of the reason he was here. Her voice—his eyes dropped—her legs and, yes, her mouth.

'Will you stop that? It isn't funny,' she croaked crossly.

His glance moved upwards to the full soft pink contours of her lips. Yes, they had all been factors—they and the fact he thought that the sexy and stuck-up Dr Semple needed to be taught a lesson. You really shouldn't judge by appearances.

'Of course what you actually say isn't always riveting,' he conceded in an attitude of regret as he ducked to enter the bedroom. He looked around with interest.

'Not bad!' He walked over to the canopied half tester and patted the mattress. 'Firm, but I like that.'

Megan responded to the fact he was looking at her body and not the bed when he said this with an irritated air. Actually she would have welcomed some irritation at that moment, if he said the things his seductive eyes managed to convey he could probably be arrested.

He fell back onto the bed and, crossing one leg over the

other, tucked his hands behind his head so that he could look at her. 'Where's your room?'

'Next door,' she admitted reluctantly.

'Handy.'

Her eyes narrowed. 'The moment you begin to believe that, you're out of here.'

To her intense annoyance he seemed to find her threat wildly amusing. Maybe, she thought darkly, it was the idea of any woman saying no to him that struck him as funny…?

'My mother is a firm believer in propinquity. I am not,' she told him drily. 'Perhaps we should lay down a few ground rules.'

'I should tell you I'm not big on rules,' he confided, stifling a yawn.

'Now there's a surprise.'

'In fact,' he admitted. 'I see a rule and I feel this almost overwhelming desire to bend it a little,' he returned, stretching with languid grace.

Megan felt her stomach muscles clench and looked at him in frustration. Without trying he could drive her crazy. What was going to happen if he took it into his head to try? It didn't bear thinking about.

Her expression fixed she braced her hand on the back of a chair covered in faded tapestry. One day she might be able to work out why she had ever thought this was a good idea. Right now that day seemed awfully far off.

'Why am I getting the idea you're not taking this seriously…?'

'I get the idea you take everything much *too* seriously,' he retorted, looking at her curiously. 'What do you do when you're not looking down a microscope?'

'I avoid men like you.' Actually she had never met a man like him. Were there any other men like him…?

'Have you seen the ghost?'

Her eyes narrowed suspiciously. 'How do you know we have a ghost?' she wanted to know.

'Don't all old places like this have a ghost...or several...?'

'I suppose they do,' she admitted. 'But I've never seen one.' And frankly a ghost would scare her less than this incredibly sexy man did. 'Now, seriously, we should lay down some ground rules.'

His head went back, revealing his strong brown throat as he laughed. Oh, God, she thought, he really is just too attractive, in a dangerous what-the-hell-is-he-going-to-do-next sort of way.

'Right, forget the rules, just keep it simple. If in doubt say nothing; better still, let me do all the talking.'

'Won't that make me appear as if I don't have an opinion of my own?'

'That's the way I like my men.'

'Under your thumb.' He extended his aforementioned digit towards her.

He had nice hands, she noticed, but then he had nice everything. 'I like the strong, silent type...' she crisply corrected. 'If in doubt just look enigmatic,' she advised. Her frown deepened as she scanned his face. 'Do you think you could do that?'

'I could.'

'But are you going to do?' Or was he going to make a total fool out of her?

'Is this suitably enigmatic...?'

'You're a natural,' she assured him drily. This was all going to go terribly wrong.

'Relax,' he advised. 'This is going to be fun.'

'If you think this is fun you have a seriously warped mind. Now just try and remember,' she pleaded, 'you're a famous author.'

'I'm a famous author,' he repeated solemnly. 'Do you believe me?'

'I know you're not...I don't count.'

'Believe me, by the end of tonight I'll be so good even you will believe I'm a famous author.'

'Let's not get too ambitious.' She glanced at her watch. 'I've got to get changed for dinner.' She extended one denim-covered leg to prove the point. 'I'll come back for you in half an hour. Don't,' she added, wagging a warning finger at him, 'move until I get here.'

Of course he did.

CHAPTER FIVE

THE French doors had been open all through dinner and the guests had drifted out onto the terrace to sip their drinks and chat. Despite the unpromising start the day had produced a perfect summer evening, warm and balmy, spoilt only by an unexpected shower, which was brief but heavy.

Luc and Megan were caught out in the open when the heavens opened. By the time they reached the shelter offered by the leafy canopy of the ancient oak tree it had stopped raining.

Luc, grinning, shook his head, sending droplets of water everywhere. 'There's something exhilarating about a summer shower.'

Easy for him to say, she thought.

Casting a resentful glance from under her lashes at Luc's classically perfect profile, she pondered the unfairness that made him look incredible with his hair plastered damply to his skull. The moisture that clung to his naturally dark skin only served to emphasise the healthy glow.

She had gone for a vintage look tonight. With a sigh she looked down with distaste at her silk calf-length skirt; it clung damply to her legs. The chiffon overskirt with its beading detail might well be ruined—pity, it had been her favourite. She could feel the excess moisture from her wet hair running in a cold trickle down her neck, she didn't even want to think about what it looked like.

Luc, his back set against the gnarled tree trunk, watched as she ran her hands down her bare arms to remove the excess moisture that clung to her pale smooth skin. She had great arms; like the rest of her body they were toned and firm.

At least the cotton halter-top wouldn't be ruined by the rain, Megan thought, concentrating on the positive. Which was more than could be said for her hair...negative thoughts refused to be *totally* banished.

'Have you ever danced?'

A line forming between her feathery brows, Megan lifted her head to look at the tall figure standing in the shadows. '*Dance?* What on earth are you talking about?' She glared up at him, bristling with suspicion.

Luc registered the antagonistic glitter in her eyes, but didn't comment on it. 'You're very graceful.'

Megan felt her cheeks grow hot. 'Don't be ridiculous.'

'I was simply making an observation. You carry yourself like a dancer. I was wondering if you trained at some point...?'

'Me, a dancer!' She looked at him as though he had gone mad. 'I'm a research scientist.'

'Does being a boffin preclude you having a sense of rhythm?'

She dealt him a look of exasperation. 'I don't dance. I...well, I did have a few lessons when I was a kid,' she conceded. 'Singing lessons too. They were meant to help my asthma.'

'Did they?'

'Well, it got a lot better.'

'You're shivering,' he observed as a fresh shudder ran visibly through her slender frame. 'I'd offer you a jacket except...' his grin made him appear almost impossibly attractive '...I'm not wearing one.'

Megan watched him place his hand flat against his chest. A shaft of agonising awareness shot through her—she was conscious of every crease and fold of the white cotton that clung like a second skin to the broad expanse of his chest. She was even more painfully conscious of the shadow of body hair sprinkled over his broad chest and the suggestion of muscular definition.

Drawing a deep breath as she struggled to regain her composure, Megan developed a deep interest in his shoes.

'You can have my shirt if you like.'

Her stomach flipped over at the thought of wearing something that was still warm from his skin, something that still bore the scent of his body.

An awful thought occurred to her. Did he know that she had just been mentally removing it? Had she been *that* obvious?

'I don't like.' It wasn't just cold that made her teeth chatter violently, it was images of Luc standing there stripped to the waist, his golden skin gleaming his... Stop this, Megan! This was not the time or place to explore her darker emotions!

'Do you want to go back to the house?' she asked him abruptly.

'What's wrong with you?' Luc enquired, scanning her rigid face.

After his performance tonight Megan couldn't believe he had the cheek to ask. Of course she had known when she had gone back to his room and found it empty that she had made a terrible mistake. When she had come downstairs and found him surrounded by a laughing, admiring crowd who were hanging on his every word all her worst fears had been realised.

'Nothing's wrong with *me*.' She sniffed.

'I thought tonight went very well.'

Megan released a laugh of bitter incredulity at this self-congratulatory comment. 'I noticed you were enjoying yourself.'

It would have been hard to miss it!

And to think she had been concerned that he might find himself a little out of his depth during dinner. The gathering had been typical of her mother's weekends. A diplomat, a poet and his lawyer wife, an actress...least said about the voluptuous Hilary, the better! A retired headmaster, and someone who had written a number one rock ballad, then entered politics.

Far from being out of his depth, her fake lover had been totally at ease. His ability to converse on a wide range of subjects with authority and ease had astounded her and impressed the hell out of everyone else.

Of course she had already known that he was intelligent. Two seconds in his company revealed that. Now she knew that, though he might have no formal education to speak of, he was widely read and amazingly erudite with a sharp wit and deadly charm. Her lips pursed; the recollection of his *deadly* charm reminded her of how angry she was.

'Come on, let's walk in the sun. It might warm you up.'

'I'm not cold,' she denied, wrapping her arms around her trembling body.

'Well, I am.'

After a short pause she followed him back out into the evening sun.

'Are you going to tell me what I've done to make you mad?'

'You need to ask?'

'I just did.'

'It might have slipped your memory that the reason—the *only* reason you are here is to establish that you find me irresistible. It might be a start if you had deigned to notice I was alive,' she ground out grimly.

Until he had asked her to take this stroll outside he had acted as though she were invisible. If she hadn't wanted to get him alone long enough to give him a piece of her mind, she'd have told him where he could stick his stroll!

His dark shapely brows moved towards his equally dark and at that moment damp hairline. 'I haven't forgotten why I'm here.'

Megan's lips tightened. His dismissive attitude really got under her skin. 'So ignoring me and spending the entire evening talking to someone else's cleavage is your idea of seeming interested? *Interesting technique,'* she admired with heavy sarcasm.

The memory of his humiliating fascination with the actress's breasts increased the angry tightness in her aching throat. She'd probably hear that woman's awful laugh in her sleep tonight, she decided, thinking of the shrill, jarring sound. Why was it that every single time men went for *obvious*...?

Not, of course, that she gave a damn if he fancied the redhead—after all, that hardly placed him in a unique category. Hilary was the sort of woman who demanded and got male attention. No, Megan's legitimate grouch was the fact he wasn't fulfilling his end of the bargain. Her acting as an introduction agent for him, a fact she had every intention of pointing out, was not part of the deal.

For a moment her angry eyes met his before her lashes swept downwards and she turned and backed away.

'Calm down, *chérie.*' He laughed, catching her arm and swinging her back.

Her shrill, 'I am calm!' made him laugh again.

'Not so as you'd notice.' The first time he'd seen her he'd wondered what she would look like without her upper-crust reserve intact and he had had ample opportunity to find out today. 'Unreasonable and ratty is actually not a bad look for you.'

Something in his voice brought Megan's eyes back to his face. 'I am neither unreasonable nor ratty!' She regarded him with simmering dislike. 'I just don't like wasting my time,' she enunciated clearly.

'I haven't been wasting anything.'

His patronising tone made her teeth clench. 'Certainly no opportunity to chat up anything in a low-cut top.' And if he thought that cleavage was natural he was in for a nasty shock.

'What we've established tonight is that you mind me showing an interest in another woman.'

His smugness made Megan want to scream.

'Your reaction was perfect,' he commended calmly.

'I didn't react,' she told him frigidly. Actually, now that she reviewed her behaviour during the interminable dinner, she had to concede that maybe her conduct hadn't been quite as adult as it might have been, but, in her defence, she had had a lot of provocation.

'God, and to think I thought you had no sense of humour. Everyone there was aware of the friction.'

Megan inhaled deeply. '*Friction…?*' she parroted.

Her cheeks turned a deeper pink as she looked significantly at the long brown fingers still curled over her bare upper arm. The fingers stayed where they were. God, but he had to be the most insensitive, thick-skinned man she had ever had the misfortune to encounter! The idea of respecting personal space was obviously a foreign concept to him.

Megan decided to bravely rise above it all. Rather than participate in an unseemly struggle, she forced herself to stand there passively even though his fingers felt like a white-hot brand against her skin.

'You would have said black if I had said white. In fact I'm not sure you didn't!' he added wryly. 'But don't worry—like I said, that's no problem. We're going to have a turbulent relationship—a classic case of opposites attracting. I predict a lot of really epic rows in public and some epic making up too.'

'If you try to make up with me you'll end up in traction,' she promised. 'And actually opposites don't attract, they end up making each other miserable. And just for the record,' she added grimly, 'I realise that you think you're God's gift, but, trust me—the only thing I minded tonight was not being given value for money.'

'Well, let me remind you, *chérie*, that you haven't bought me.' His narrowed gaze suddenly turned molten silver as he scanned her angry upturned features. 'You're giving me

something I want and I'm giving you something you want…
or I could if you let me.'

The suggestive drawl in his deep, musical voice sent a
surge of heat through Megan's rigid frame.

'That remains to be seen,' she gulped. Unable to bear the
contact for another moment without crawling clear out of
her skin, she tugged her arm free of his clasp. 'And don't
keep calling me *chérie*! I am not your darling and I have a
name,' she said, standing there rubbing the invisible imprint
of his fingers on her flesh.

'And claws…' he observed in a soft, sibilant voice that
made the invisible downy hairs on her skin stand erect.

Luc's silvered glance touched her small hands, which
now hung tensely at her sides, balled tightly into fists. Her
incredible eyes, shadowed in the fading light, were fixed on
his face and her body language screamed hostility.

Against all the odds he experienced a surge of protective warmth. The reaction was inexplicable, but amazingly
strong.

'Chemistry, like ours, usually produces a few sparks…a
lot if you're lucky,' he added as an amused afterthought.

'Not for me it doesn't,' Megan rebutted firmly. She
frowned. She hoped he wasn't forgetting this was all make
believe. It would be very embarrassing if she had to remind
him.

Her frown deepened.

'You don't like sparks…?'

She didn't smile in response to his teasing tone, but looking at him standing there, so incredibly gorgeous, made her
more conscious of the curious little ache, actually not so
little, inside her. If she was honest not so curious considering he was just about just about the most attractive man
on the planet.

'I'm not a combustible person,' she told him before con-
sulting the slim watch on her wrist. She had no intention of
apologising just because she wasn't some sort of smoulder-

ing sex bomb like Hilary. 'We ought to be heading back, people will be wondering where we've got to.'

He smiled thinly. 'They're meant to wonder what we're up to. It's all part of my master plan.'

'Don't you think under the circumstances you ought to consult me about your master plan?' she queried tartly.

'What, and lose the advantage of surprise?'

'Surprise?' she repeated, a groove appearing above the bridge of her nose as she worriedly pondered his meaning.

'You're really not a very good actress.'

'That's because deceit doesn't come as easily to me as it does to you,' she retorted. 'And,' she added, 'I don't think I want to be surprised…actually, I *know* I don't want to be surprised, especially by you.' Fortunately Luc didn't appear to have registered her unwise addition.

'Don't worry, I can think on my feet. I'm actually thought to be quite good at improvising.'

'It's the thought of you improvising that worries me.'

He slanted her an amused look. Megan pursed her lips and glared back coldly. She couldn't share his light-hearted approach; this fly-by-the-seat-of-your-pants thing just wasn't her. Unlike him she wasn't the type of person who got a buzz from living close to the edge. The constant fear of being caught out didn't give her an adrenaline rush, just a sick feeling of dread in the pit of her stomach.

'There is one thing I wouldn't mind knowing…' he admitted with a frown.

The corners of his sensually sculpted lips twitched as his glance dropped. 'You're not a bad-looking woman…' came the verdict after several uncomfortable moments.

Megan batted her eyelashes. 'Wow, thanks!'

Underneath the gushing insincerity she was badly spooked by the way her body instantly reacted to his slow, insolent perusal. Could you class the strength leaving your shaking lower limbs and the ignition of a hot burning flame deep in your belly as *spooked*? Or was it something more serious? She was thinking terminal blind lust here...

The acid interjection brought an answering flicker of humour to his deep-set eyes but didn't deflect him from his purpose.

'So I'm assuming that there are men in your life.'

Megan was continually amazed and *increasingly* aggravated by his apparent belief that being a co-conspirator gave him the right to delve into all personal aspects of her life. She watched his expression grow reflective as he focused his thoughts on the subject of her love life.

'Men compose half the population; it would be hard to avoid them even if I wanted to.'

Luc acted as though she hadn't spoken—something she had noticed he had a habit of doing—as he continued. 'But you don't bring them home to meet Mummy. Now I wonder why...?' One dark brow elevated he turned his speculative gaze upon her face. *'Married...?'*

Megan stiffened in outrage. 'You th...th...think that I would go out with a m...m...married man?' she demanded.

Luc silently studied her rigid chalk white features for a moment before shrugging. 'Apparently not,' he observed drily. 'I've got a mate...your classic commitment phobic who only dates married women. I thought that might be your problem.'

'That you have that sort of mate does not surprise me.'

'He's a reformed character since he met the love of his life. So if they're not married...what's the problem? Not the right social class? Don't they know which fork to use?'

The amazing thing was he didn't even seem to be aware he'd insulted her!

Megan fixed him with a look of seething dislike. If she still had some of the power that the ancestors he despised had enjoyed and, she was the first to admit, abused, she would have wielded them in this instance.

Contemplating having him shipped off to some distant colony, preferably one infested by insects that would bite his smooth, sleek hide, brought a grim smile to her lips. As she contemplated the vee of smooth olive-toned skin visible at the base of his throat her smile wobbled.

For some reason she found herself thinking about an infamous female ancestor of hers. The scandalous Lady Edith who was reputed to have enjoyed the services of several lusty local lads, one of whom was said to have fathered her son who had inherited the estate. Edith, with her shameless appetites, would have had different methods of taming a stroppy male. She would have undoubtedly considered the banishment of Luc, with his sleek, dark and incredibly sexy looks, a waste.

Edith would have found a place for him in her bed.

'Does a bit of rough do it for you?'

The disturbing mental image of Luc tumbling amongst silk sheets with the sloe-eyed lady who looked down haughtily from a painting in the library vanished in a flash. Megan released a long sibilant hiss of fury.

'Go jump in the lake,' she urged pleasantly.

Luc grinned at her venom. 'It's a reasonable question,' he protested.

'My personal life is none of your business,' she told him frigidly.

'It is if you have a secret boyfriend hovering in the background somewhere,' Luc retorted. 'If someone is likely to try and knock my lights out I'd like to know about it.'

She gave a disdainful laugh. 'So this is about you being scared, is it? I should have known,' she sneered scornfully.

He sighed. 'My secret is out.'

'Well, you can relax. Your pretty profile is not in any danger.' Actually he looked, in stark contrast to herself, totally relaxed, especially considering the barrage of abuse she was aiming at his dark head.

'No jealous boyfriend lurking...?'

She half turned then with a hard laugh flung over her shoulder.

'No boyfriend full stop. And before you progress to the painfully predictable male, *you-must-be-a-lesbian* line…I'm not.' She stopped dead and frowned. 'I've not the faintest idea why I'm explaining myself to you,' she admitted angrily.

His shoulders lifted. 'Don't look at me, but go on—I'm finding it educational.'

Megan fixed him with a narrowed resentful glare. It was actually good advice—*looking at him,*…even hearing his deep drawl, was a recipe for stress and mental disintegration.

'I have no time for a boyfriend. As I have already told you, at this point in my life I want to concentrate all my energies on my career.' It made Megan so furious, if she had been a man her decision would not have caused any raised eyebrows.

'*And…*' he prompted when she stayed silent.

'There is no *and*,' she told him crossly.

'A love life or a career is not generally considered an either-or decision.'

'For me they are.'

'Aren't women meant to be big on multitasking?'

'That rumour was undoubtedly started by a man who was more than happy for his partner to run herself ragged trying to do all the things he didn't have time for.'

Luc looked amused. 'You could be right, but you were engaged so you couldn't always have felt that way.'

Unconsciously Megan's hand went to her cheek.

'How did you know about Brian?'

'Your mother told me; she was pretty gutted that you chucked him.'

'She got over it.' Frankly she didn't care if he thought she was a cold, heartless bitch.

'No job is a substitute for sex.'

The way Brian did it, it was. 'Did I say I was celibate?'

His brows lifted sardonically. 'Your mother thinks you are.'

Megan flushed. 'This is the twenty-first century, Luc,' she told him, injecting scorn into her voice. 'Does everything have to be about sex?' *When did I start panting?* Megan pressed a hand to her throat and made a concerted effort to slow the shallow, rapid character of her breathing.

Knuckles pressed to the slight indent in his chin, Luc pretended to consider the matter. 'Yes.' Eyes that seemed scarily *knowing* zeroed in on her face.

Now she wasn't just panting as if she'd been running a marathon, she was sweating too. *Did everybody find his mouth as fascinating as she did?* Megan wondered as she watched one corner drop in a cynical smirk.

'Few things in life are constant, but sex is,' he contended in a throaty purr that ought in a fair world to have been preceded by a 'there are flashing lights in this film' type warning for the susceptible.

Megan was definitely susceptible! The moisture between her aching thighs was ample evidence of that.

'It doesn't really matter what decade or, for that matter, what century; it doesn't change. Scratch the surface of the most sophisticated male and you'll find a man who is thinking about sex. Take me, for instance…'

This smooth suggestion wrenched an instinctive croak of protest from Megan's throat. He angled a questioning brow at her flushed, uncomfortable face.

'I don't think I will, if it's all the same to you. You may be right about men, they probably haven't evolved beyond the Neanderthal, but women—of course, I can only speak personally—can rise above their hormones. We've learnt how to work the system like men have been doing for years. A man doesn't date a woman with the primary intention of settling down and starting a family. Why should it be different for a woman?'

'So you're telling me that any sexual needs you have are satisfied by no-strings one-night stands.'

Megan wasn't, she had been blustering, but she was quite prepared to take the credit for this idea. In reality the idea of emotionless sex was not something she warmed to, but he didn't need to know that.

'You have a problem with that?' she gritted belligerently.

'Men and women are driven by very different biological needs. A man has the basic urge to impregnate a woman, to nurture.'

'That's remarkably sexist…' But sadly probably essentially true…is that me talking or my conditioning? In the end does it really matter? I am, and I don't do casual sex.

'No, that's a biological fact,' he stated bluntly. 'I'd say if you try to act like a man you stand every chance of being badly hurt.'

'On the contrary it's women who fall in love with men and idolise them who get hurt when they…' Aware that her comment had awakened a speculative gleam in his eyes she checked her emotional flow abruptly and began to examine her linked fingers.

'Who did you idolise?'

'We were all young and stupid once.'

The silence between them lengthened.

'What's through there?'

Relieved that he had dropped the subject, she turned and saw him lifting the latch on a tall wrought-iron gate half hidden in the ivy-covered wall.

'It's an entrance to the workshops,' she replied absently, 'but this isn't the way back to the house. Where are you going now?'

'What's the hurry?' he asked, skimming her a questioning look before pushing the gate open to reveal a courtyard.

CHAPTER SIX

MEGAN followed Luc into the attractive flower-bedecked courtyard, her heels clicking loudly on the wet cobbled surface. 'It used to be the old stables.'

'And now it's...?'

'A bit of a tourist attraction.' She saw him lift his hand to his eyes to peer into the darkened window of the forge. 'That's Sam's studio.'

'Sam...?'

'He was a bus driver, now he makes terrific wrought-iron stuff to order.'

A local potter had approached her father ten years earlier with a view to him renting her workspace. The idea had snowballed...

'And the others...?' Luc's expansive gesture took in the rest of the quadrangle.

'There are about ten workshops here now all used by local artists and craftsmen,' she told him proudly. 'They double as workspace and a shop front. There's a really marvellous community feel about the place. People can come and watch them work and, if they like it, buy what they see. There are also occasional workshops where you can learn to throw a pot, that sort of thing. Local schools frequently come. It's proved rather successful.'

So much so that the planning authorities were considering an application to extend the operation into the adjoining granary providing tearooms and an art gallery.

'Very enterprising.'

'It's a non-profit-making operation,' she added defensively. Wanting to gain his approval just a little too much. 'We charge a nominal rent and—'

'Hold up,' he interrupted. 'I may think the aristocracy is an anachronism in this day and age, but that doesn't mean I assume that they are *all* out to subjugate the masses.

'That's remarkably open-minded of you, L...'

'Luc,' he prompted, watching with a glimmer of a smile in his deep-set eyes as she bit her lip. 'It is my name.'

'You don't have to *live* the role you—' She broke off and gave a grimace as a stab of pain shot through her right ankle.

'Are you all right?'

Megan waved aside his concern and flexed her right foot. 'Fine, just turned my ankle, that's all.' She frowned at the heel that had got jammed in a crevice in the uneven cobbled surface. She pulled but it didn't budge. She swore softly under her breath. 'These things are lethal,' she complained.

'But very sexy.' His lashes lifted and the glitter she saw reflected in the platinum depths of his eyes made her heart thud.

Flushing, Megan lowered her gaze and let the skirt she was holding, gathered bunched in her hand, fall with a damp, silken slither to the ground.

'I'm not prepared to cripple myself in the pursuit of wolf-whistles...*normally*,' she added drily.

Megan had no self-esteem issue, she knew that some men found her attractive, but even while she had been carefully selecting her outfit earlier she had been aware that, no matter what she wore, it wasn't going to make her look drop-dead gorgeous. It was a fact of life that men who looked like Luc were not generally seen with women who looked the way she did, so tonight she had made an effort.

'I haven't inherited my mother's fashion sense or, for that matter, her figure.' Forgetting for a split second whom she was talking to, she pressed her hands flat to her nicely formed but not impressive bosom.

Luc's eyes followed her gesture and his lips twitched. There was no hint of apology in her gesture, just the merest suggestion of wistfulness. 'You look fine to me.'

The notion that he might have thought she had been fishing for compliments brought a deep flush to her fair skin and a look of horror to her face.

'I can do without your approval.' Do without, but wouldn't it be nice to have it…? Megan's glance dropped as the thought surfaced unbidden to her mind.

His heavy sigh—a mixture of resignation and irritation, brought her head up.

Eyes holding hers, he set his shoulders against the wall behind him. With his weight braced on one leg, he crossed one ankle over the other. The man, she admitted, could slouch like nobody else she had ever met.

'Do you actually want this thing to work?'

The question startled her out of her contemplation of his effortlessly elegant body language. 'Of course I want this to work. Why wouldn't I?'

His lips formed a twisted smile as he scanned her face. 'Good question. Well, if you do want a result it's going to require a bit of effort.'

Effort? Did he have any idea how much effort she was making? 'What do you mean "effort"?'

'Well, for starters you're going to have to put some work in on the adoring love slave front…'

The awful Brian had expected if not demanded his bride-to-be's uncritical adoration as his due, and he had received it. That was, until Megan had woken up to the fact that he was an inadequate creep, and furthermore she didn't love him. Megan fixed Luc with a glare and tossed her head, a disdainful sneer twisting her lips.

'What's wrong with your face?' he asked, watching her rub the left side of her face. His eyes narrowed; it wasn't the first time he had noticed her doing that. The first time had been…when…?

Megan's hand fell self-consciously away. She tried to turn but her foot held her fast. 'Damn…damn,' she cursed.

'Did he hit you?'

An expression of total shock chased across her pale features as she focused on his face. His expression was blank.

It wasn't the reminder of that contemptuous backhander that Brian had delivered when she had explained that she would not be giving up her job or marrying him that brought the look of dismay to her face, but this man's startling perception. It was almost as if he could read her mind at times.

'Pardon…?' she faltered.

'You heard me,' he intoned grimly.

'Once,' she admitted, because one look at his face revealed he wasn't going to let this one go.

Brian had said it wouldn't happen again, but Megan had seen the mask slip and had recognised his tearful apology for the lie it had been. In a weird way it had been a relief; it had been much easier to walk away with a clear conscience.

Luc struggled to keep his expression neutral; it wasn't easy. He couldn't remember the last time he had felt anything like this sort of blinding rage, this desire to rip someone limb from limb, and laugh while he was doing it.

'Why didn't you tell your mother the scumbag hit you? She talked like he was the second coming.'

'It would have upset her and…I suppose I was… ashamed—? Irrational, I know, but I'm not a victim.'

For a long painful moment Luc looked down into her face. His shoulders lifted. 'No, just a stubborn idiot,' he gritted. 'Not all men are vicious bullies.'

'Oh, God, I know that!' she exclaimed. 'Don't run away with the impression I'm emotionally scarred or anything. Damn, damn thing…' she addressed her curse to her shoe.

'What are you doing?' Her voice was high-pitched with alarm as he hunkered down in front of her. She stiffened as Luc took hold of her ankle. Megan swayed like a sapling caught in a strong gust of wind then, eyes half closed, mouth slightly open, she took a series of shallow breaths and she forced herself to remain still.

'This situation requires a light touch.'

Well, he had that, she was forced to concede as slither after shivery slither of sensation sliced like a knife through her helplessly receptive body. It was no longer possible for her to ignore the heat, specifically the heat between her thighs. When his fingertips brushed against the fine, almost invisible denier that covered the skin of her calf she had to bite her lip to stop herself gasping out loud. The situation made it hard to think straight—actually, it made it hard to think full stop!

'It's stuck fast,' came his oddly muffled verdict after a few moments.

The dull thud in her ears made his voice seem to come from a long way off to Megan.

'Tell me something I didn't know,' she grunted, trying desperately to marshal her thoughts.

The man kneeling at her feet lifted his head. In the fading light she didn't see the lines of darker colour scoring his high slashing cheekbones, she could just see his eyes…and his mouth and…*oh, God*—!

'You should take them off.'

Anything you say. God, please let me not have said that out loud! She ran the tip of her tongue nervously over her dry lips. 'What…?' she croaked.

'The shoes,' he replied. 'You should take them off. The stockings too,' he added as an afterthought.

'How did you know?' She stopped and shook her head blushing deeply. Far better, under the circumstances, *not* to know how he knew when a woman was wearing stockings and not tights.

'Don't worry, I don't have X-ray vision.'

'I wasn't worried.' The knot of heat low in her belly made it hard for her to concentrate on what she was doing and a second later she found herself standing in one shoe, teetering awkwardly to one side without having any clear recollection of how she had got to be in that position.

'For God's sake…' His voice impatient, Luc caught her hands in his and placed them firmly on his own shoulders. 'Hold onto me.'

It was either that or fall down in an ungainly heap.

'Give me a minute,' she heard him say. 'That's it.' Hazily she saw him rise, her shoe minus the heel in his triumphant grasp. 'The shoe's a write-off, I'm afraid.'

She shook her head; the loss of a shoe was the least of her problems! Her response to this man was less easy to dismiss. In the gathering dusk it was impossible to read the expression on his lean, hard-boned face.

'It doesn't matter.' Awkwardness made her voice abrupt. Minus her heels she only just topped his shoulders. The illusion of being small and dainty was one she shouldn't in this enlightened age of equality have found attractive…*Shouldn't…!*

The impressive shoulders on which her hands were still hanging, quite unnecessarily, flexed and she felt the powerful muscles clench.

She uncurled her fingers. As if reluctant to lose the contact, her fingertips trailed slowly down the front of his open necked shirt. She felt his lean, hard body tense before she lost contact. It made her cringe to imagine that her action might have been interpreted as deliberately provocative, because she had no control whatever over her actions.

'I suppose we ought to go back.' The thread of reluctance she heard in her own voice made Megan's eyes widen in alarm. Anyone listening would have been excused for assuming she wanted her pulse to carry on racing too fast…that she wanted to prolong the moment.

And you don't…?

'You could be right.' she heard him concede. 'Do you always do the right thing, *ma chérie…*?'

Just this once Megan let the endearment pass, when he said it in that deep smoky voice of his it sounded like a caress.

With a sigh she lifted her head, her eyes meshed with enigmatic silvered orbs that made her heart pound slow and strong… Luc; the name might be no more real than his supposed attraction for her, but strangely fitted him.

He really was the most incredible-looking man!

'I try to.' She gave a shaky little laugh as her eyes slid from his. 'I won't waste my breath asking you the same thing.'

Luc looked like a man for whom *not* doing the right thing was one of life's guiding principles. Was the danger part of his attraction? Had she been playing it safe for so long that she couldn't resist what was dark, dangerous and available?

'I try to do what comes naturally.' His explanation was not soothing. 'We should definitely go back, only first…' Luc's dark head bent as he framed her face between his hands. She felt his breath fan her cheek as he fitted his mouth to hers. Megan's eyelashes fluttered against her cheek as her hand came up to cover one of his.

She murmured his name; the sound was lost against his mouth. The pressure of his lips was gentle but insistent; his mouth was cool and firm against her own.

Luc drew back, his lashes lifted from the angle of his knife-edged cheekbones as he examined the passion-flushed features of the woman who stood in the circle of his arms. He gave an almost imperceptible nod of satisfaction.

'*Now* you look like a woman who's shared a few illicit kisses in the moonlight.'

She was floating; she was on fire, every inch of her skin was prickling with the heat of desire. His words had the same effect as an icy shower.

'There is no moon and I will not be used by you or anyone else!' she declared in a low, passionate voice.

'I wasn't using you; I was kissing you and,' he added with a slow, contemplative smile, 'I was enjoying it.'

'How nice for you that you're happy in your work. Next time maybe you might like to ask whether I *want* to be kissed,' she told him, dragging a hand across her mouth. The symbolic gesture just reminded her of how sensitised and tender her lips felt.

Luc, no longer languid, looked suddenly incredibly furious. 'Are you suggesting I kissed you against your will?'

'Not *exactly*,' she conceded, her glance dropping guiltily from his outraged face.

'Good,' he bit back, not sounding much mollified. 'Because I don't need a signed affidavit to know when a woman wants to be kissed. I know and you wanted it.'

The shocking sound of her hand connecting with his cheek resounded across the courtyard. Megan's hand went to her mouth as her eyes travelled from the livid mark developing on his lean cheek to his eyes, they told her nothing more than his blank expression.

'That was unforgivable,' she said, totally contrite. The fact that physically she was much weaker than him was in her eyes no excuse for her loss of control. She felt deeply ashamed. 'You're right.' Humiliation sat like a leaden weight in her stomach. 'I *did* want you to kiss me.'

'You did?'

She nodded; his expression was as unrevealing as his tone. 'That's why I was so angry…not with you,' she hastened to assure him. 'With me.'

It was ironic—she had been busy getting het up worrying that Luc was getting too immersed in his role, when in reality *he* wasn't the one getting reality mixed up with fiction; she was the one letting her fantasies take control!

Luc watched as her slender shoulders sagged.

'Obviously this thing is not going to work; it's not your fault.' Luc, after all, had done everything she had asked of him. 'It's me.'

'You wanted me to kiss you…?' A muscle in his hollow cheek clenched.

Megan looked at him, her frustration showing. Had he not heard anything she had said after that? She hoped he had; she didn't much fancy grovelling all over again. In fact she refused to, she decided with a spurt of defiance.

'Well, I wasn't exactly averse to it,' she admitted gruffly. 'I appreciate you were doing what you thought I wanted.'

'I was doing what I *hoped* you wanted,' he contradicted, sliding his hands down her slender back until they came to rest on the firm curve of her bottom. His grin flashed out minus the edge of cool dispassion and mockery she had grown accustomed to. 'Now I know...'

'Know what?' She gave a startled gasp as he drew her towards him until their hips collided. She inhaled sharply as hot desire zapped through her body; he was rock-hard against the softness of her belly. An energising wave zapped through her body, her knees sagged and Luc took up the slack ably, wrapping one strong arm around her ribcage.

'Know you want this.' He ground his hips gently against her abdomen. Megan's head fell back bonelessly as the silent groan locked in her tight throat struggled to escape. Mutely, she nodded. Not pretending any more, felt strangely liberating.

His big hand cupped the back of her skull, drawing her face up to his. Looking into his platinum-grey eyes made her dizzy.

'This is quite spectacularly crazy.'

She tried to swallow but couldn't. She couldn't stop shaking, tremors that ran like febrile shudders through her entire body. Insane it might be, but she could actually *feel* his voice. No man had ever excited her this way...up until now she had thought she wasn't capable of feeling this way. What if it never happened again?

The thought spurred her into direct action. 'I don't do crazy, Luc.' Her lashes lifted and she looked him straight in the eyes. 'But I could learn.'

Luc's nostrils flared as he sucked in a startled gasp.

CHAPTER SEVEN

MEGAN'S head dropped. God, she'd been too direct...she'd shocked Luc and small wonder! Her comment had been only slightly less subtle than screaming, *Take me!* Just because you fancy the socks off him doesn't mean he feels the same way!

Teeth clenched, she resisted the hand that curved under her chin and his soft but firm instruction, 'Look at me, Megan.' Until finally with an exasperated sigh she allowed her face to be tilted up to his.

The mixture of embarrassment and defiance faded from her face as she looked at him. He was smiling a smile so fierce so sweet that she felt as if she'd melt. His fingertips ran along the curve of her jaw and she turned her head into his hand and kissed his palm.

'I'll teach you,' he rasped.

This time there was nothing vaguely tentative or gentle about his lips or the probing tongue that slid between her parted lips. Electrified, Megan kissed him back with a driven desperation. Whimpering softly into his mouth, she wound her arms tightly around his neck.

Her mind had stopped functioning. She was simply responding to the primitive need that made her plaster her aching breasts against his chest, pressing her hips into his. She couldn't get close enough to him. She had no idea of how long they stood there kissing with a frenzied, frantic desperation.

At some point they must have stopped kissing long enough to end up standing beneath the porch of one of the stable workshops.

'My God, don't stop!' she pleaded, her self-control a dim

66

and distant memory by the time his mouth lifted from her own. She lifted her dazed, passion-glazed eyes to his dark face. 'You're…I feel…' She struggled to articulate the hunger that coursed like a forest fire through her body.

'My God, but you're incredible,' he breathed, scanning her face with blazing eyes.

Megan felt his hand slide under her skirt at the same time her back made contact with the ivy-covered wall. His heavy, warm body pressed her into the hard surface.

'Oh, my God!' she groaned, biting her lip.

She felt the pressure ease. 'Am I hurting you?' he asked thickly.

Megan slid her hands under his shirt across his satiny hard skin. She released a shuddering sigh as the muscles contracted under her questing fingers. She felt him suck in a deep breath as the fabric parted. Squirming, she pressed her aching breasts against his bare flesh.

She ran the tip of her tongue over the outline of her swollen lips. 'You're killing me.'

A low feral groan that made her hot skin break out in a rash of goosebumps emerged from Luc's throat as he responded to the sexual challenge glittering in her eyes. 'That's not what I want to do to you.'

'What do you want to do?' she asked in a throaty whisper.

'This, for starters.' His fingers reached the bare skin above the lacy tops of her hold-ups and she let out a deep moan as her stomach muscles contracted violently.

'You're…you're…'

'What am I?' he prompted throatily.

Impossible to resist. Megan shook her head, the ache between her legs intensifying as her eyes dropped down the length of his incredible body. She was aware of every hard inch of him. She wanted every hard inch of him.

Megan blinked to bring his face into focus; her breath was coming in shallow, uneven gasps. The skin was drawn tight across his high cheekbones. His dark lashes lifted, revealing an almost feral glitter of raw hunger in his eyes.

'You're to die for.'

A grin of savage male triumph spread across his face. 'Not just yet, Megan,' he responded, loosing the tie of her halter top with one hand while touching the dampness between her legs with the other.

He was breathing hard and fast but Megan, who was doing the same, didn't notice. She was conscious only of the heat in her blood and Luc stroking her, driving her crazy in a beautiful, mindless way.

Yanking down the neck of her halter top to her waist, he dropped his molten gaze to the pouting contours of her small pink-tipped breasts. The cool air felt like velvet against her sensitised skin. His tongue as he moved it across each erect nipple felt like fire.

She felt like fire.

She reached for him, touching the hardness through the material of his trousers. Luc's breath started to come even faster. Megan moaned softly as she felt his hard male body surge against her hand.

After a few seconds he took her hands in his and holding them above her head, pressed her into the wall. 'I can't give you slow and sweet,' he admitted, sliding a finger inside her. Megan's body arched as she gasped and sobbed his name. The muscles in her thighs were trembling violently.

'I'll take whatever you have. So long as I feel you inside me in the next ten seconds I don't care…I don't care about anything!' she declared wildly.

'Hush,' he soothed, kissing her mouth. 'I will…I will,' he promised throatily. Megan was vaguely conscious of the sound of him adjusting his clothing as she kissed him back and told him she loved everything about him.

She felt him against her soft belly, hard and aroused; she had no time to feel concerned about *how* aroused before he thrust up into her, filling her with his thickness.

'My God,' he rasped, his breath hot against her neck. 'You're so tight.'

She was in a state of mindless pleasure as he moved inside her, slowly at first, then faster and harder the way she wanted, the way she told him she wanted. The tremors began to build inside then burst into an incredible orgasmic release just seconds before she felt Luc's hot release inside her.

They sagged to the floor together in an exhausted tangle of limbs. Utterly spent, her knees still trembling, Megan let her cheek rest against his bare chest. The whorls of dark hair tickled her nose. Luc's arms were around her, and she closed her eyes and listened to the thud of his heartbeat… Gradually it slowed to a steady thud. His skin was hot and slightly damp; the faint scent of the cologne he had used earlier mixed with the musky male scent of his body.

The intimacy was like nothing she had ever experienced in her life.

Luc placed his hand under her chin and lifted her face. Megan waited for the embarrassment she had expected to feel to surface; it didn't. The most conventional of sex with Brian had left her feeling embarrassed and always self-conscious.

'I've dreamed about doing that since the first moment I saw you,' he told her. 'But then,' he said, stroking her hair back from her face, I expect you already knew that.'

'No,' she said honestly. 'I didn't even know I wanted to do it until just now.'

Luc laughed at this disingenuous confession and got to his feet.

Shyly she took the hand he offered and let him heave her to her feet. She tilted her head back to look into his dark features. 'Is it possible to fall in love with someone you don't know?'

Immediately Luc's dark features clenched. He looked as though she had just slapped his face.

Megan gave a shaky laugh. If you could die from sheer embarrassment she would be stretched out right now. 'That was rhetorical, no answer expected or required…in case you were wondering…'

'Turn around,' he said abruptly.

Megan did as he asked and felt his fingers brush against the bare skin of her back as he fastened her halter top. She shivered and he swore softly and fumbled the knot.

'What's wrong? I didn't mean me…I…oh, God…!'

He kissed the nape of her neck, then, hands on her shoulders, spun her around. His eyes burned as though lit from within.

'What's wrong is you make me…' He made a visible effort to control himself, then with a sigh of frustration dragged a hand through his hair. 'I think it would be a good idea if we got back to the house.'

'Of course.'

As they neared the house she could hear the sound of laughter and voices; someone was playing the piano, and not very well. There was woodsmoke in the air so she assumed that the fire in the enormous grate had been lit. The drawing room with its panelled walls and views out over the lake was her favourite room but the thought of going into it now made her cringe inside. There was simply no way she could act as if nothing had happened between her and Luc.

Megan shook her head and started to back away. 'I can't go in there.'

Luc overruled her. 'Of course you can,' he said, grabbing her hand. As he was pulling her towards him the automatic sensors on the exterior light kicked in.

She began to smooth down her clothes nervously. 'I look a mess,' she fretted. 'This skirt…'

'You look gorgeous.' Megan knew she had never looked gorgeous in her life. She opened her mouth to tell him that she didn't need to hear pretty lies when her eyes collided with his.

'And don't worry about the skirt—I'll be taking it off for you as soon as we can decently make our excuses,' he promised throatily.

A shiver ran through her from the top of her head to her curling toes. Megan doubted *decency* had ever been used to describe a more indecent plan. 'You think you're going to spend the night with me?' At least her embarrassing introduction of love had not put him off totally.

'Don't you?'

She felt his hand on her cheek and her head lifted. Their eyes met, and Megan was overwhelmed, not just by the stab of sexual desire that nailed her to the spot, but by the totally unexpected tenderness in his eyes.

She felt tears prickle at the back of her eyes and blinked rapidly; her throat literally ached with emotion. This is crazy—I don't even know the man! Actually the only thing she knew for sure about him was he was a good liar...*and an even better lover.*

'I wasn't sure you'd want to...?'

'I've wanted you since the first moment I saw you.' He wound a damp honey coloured curl around one long brown finger. 'I wanted to pull you down onto the sofa and make love to you right then.'

Megan began to shake. She was still blinking in a bemused fashion when a loud, familiar voice suddenly rang out.

'There they are...'

Luc lifted his hand and waved to the figure standing at the window. 'No escape now,' he said without looking at Megan.

Her mother had obviously been waiting for them. 'Where did you two get to?' she demanded as they stepped into the hallway. She focused on her daughter and gave a wince.

'Your hair, Megan…' she rebuked with a despairing shake of her head.

'I like it that way.'

The comment brought both women's attention to Luc's face.

'You do?' Laura said in a startled voice.

Megan assumed that Luc did something to confirm his strange taste to her mother, but she didn't trust herself to check it out for herself. How could anyone look at her and not *know*? She felt as though her shame were written all over her face except that, bizarrely, she didn't feel any shame at all.

'What happened to you?'

Good question. Megan took a deep breath.

'And where are your shoes?'

'Slight mishap—we got caught in the rain,' she said, lifting a self-conscious hand to her tousled head. 'I'll go and fix this.' If only other things could be fixed with a brush and hairdryer. What had happened to caution, and why… *how* did she feel so elated?

'Never mind about that now, it's fine, come along in,' Laura urged, shepherding them across the hall. 'You'll never guess who is here…'

'Who?' Megan didn't much feel like playing guessing games or being polite to guests, but she managed to feign interest.'

Her heart just about stopped when Luc suggested silkily, 'The real Lucas…?' His hand shot out to steady Megan as she stumbled. 'Oops! Watch your step there, Megan.'

'He has such a delightfully dry sense of humour,' Laura observed.

'He is so, *so* dead,' Megan added with a fixed smile. Her reproachful eyes lifted to his face. The innocent expression she encountered was about as believable as a sincere politician. 'You won't be laughing then,' she predicted grimly as she brushed the restraining fingers from her arm.

'What did you say, darling?'

Megan lifted her voice and said in a flat monotone, 'I said he's a laugh a minute.' She ignored the rumble of soft laughter at her elbow and deliberately didn't look at him.

A second later as Laura pushed open the drawing-room door she learnt who the mystery guest was. Horror immediately froze her to the spot. Megan was no coward, but suddenly she wanted to take to her heels and run!

Her scam was about to be exposed in the most horrifying way. Would she be facing public humiliation and litigation or was the author going to see the funny side of this? Did he possess a sense of humour? It wasn't as if they had harmed his reputation—maybe he might even be flattered, as someone who looked fairly ordinary might be if they found themselves being played by Brad Pitt in the film of their life story.

It was, admittedly quite a maybe.

Megan wasn't sure if she was going to throw up or faint. She angled a quick glance at the tall man beside her. He was looking at her uncle Mal, effortlessly projecting his usual unbelievable level of cool and charisma. If she had been the author with a taste for privacy she might have considered paying Luc to be her public face, but the real Lucas Patrick might not see it quite the same way.

'Uncle Mal, this is quite a surprise.' Megan wondered why the presence of her uncle should explain her mother's suddenly bright eyes, and air of barely suppressed excitement.

The figure who had risen from his seat at the piano as they'd entered came towards her. Handsome despite his thickening middle and thinning hairline, Malcolm…looked very like his younger sister.

'Oh, yes, your uncle turned up,' her mother said, dismissing her brother with a slightly irritated shrug. 'But it was Jean Paul that I was talking about.' She drew forward with a flourish the old family friend Megan had known since she was a child.

The distinguished, silver-haired Frenchman smiled at Megan. 'You look very lovely tonight, Megan,' he said with smooth Gallic charm.

Her uncle was less smooth but also complimentary. 'Megan, my dear girl, you do look well,' he told his stricken-faced niece before his glance moved past her to the tall figure who stood with one hand lightly touching her shoulder. His smile was replaced by a look of puzzlement.

'I didn't believe it when Laura said my most famous client had turned up on her doorstep,' Malcolm remarked, shaking his head.

Megan, feeling physically sick, interposed herself between the two men in an instinctively protective gesture. She couldn't let Luc take the blame, not when this had been her idea. Two bright patches of colour appeared on her cheeks.

'I can explain…' She paused, hoping for some inspired explanation, one that would let her emerge *not* looking like a duplicitous idiot who had to bribe someone to pretend to be her boyfriend.

There was no inspiration.

'It was my idea…'

'To show me the art workshops,' Luc completed smoothly for her. Hands thrust casually in his pockets, he stepped forward.

At a time like this I can admire his bottom…I've clearly become a candidate for intensive therapy, she decided despairingly.

'The flu turned out to be just a head cold, Mal. I popped a bit of vitamin C and here I am. I've been made to feel every bit as welcome as you said I would be. All that was missing was you.'

To Luc's amusement Malcolm shifted uncomfortably from one foot to the other, looking more like a guilty schoolboy than head of one of the most successful publishing houses in the country.

'Sorry, I was…urgently, called away…business…only got back this morning. Naturally when I heard you were here…' He leaned towards the younger man and murmured, 'What the hell are you up to, Luc?'

'A very good question, Mal.' His attention drifted momentarily towards Megan. He didn't elaborate.

Megan looked from one man to the other, she pressed her fingers to her temples to relieve the growing pressure. This didn't make sense.

'You know one another…?' she said blankly.

'Of course they know one another,' said her mother, who was standing a little apart from them. She scanned her daughter's pale face with a frown. 'Are you feeling all right? Heavens you've not caught this wretched cold bug, have you?'

Megan wasn't feeling *all right*. She doubted she had ever felt less all right in her life! She lifted her gaze to Luc. 'So you are Lucas Patrick, the writer…?'

He nodded.

'Who else would he be?' Laura asked.

The man I just made love to?

'A man who needs warming up,' responded Hilary huskily. Her hungry eyes announced to everyone that it was a task she was only too willing to take on! 'You look frozen, Luc!' she purred.

Megan watched in seething silence as the voluptuous woman trailed her scarlet-painted fingers slowly down Luc's chest. She felt sick.

'You feel cold too, darling.'

Luc looked directly at Megan over the redhead's glossy head. The expression in his deep-set eyes said, *Save me!* Megan smiled back heartlessly. Save him! Hilary could eat him alive as far as she was concerned!

In the distance Megan was vaguely conscious of her

mother asking if she had had a knock on the head. Someone else suggested that what she needed was a good stiff drink to warm her up.

Good idea, Megan thought, reaching for the decanter of brandy on the bureau. In one smooth motion she filled her glass to the brim and lifted it to her lips.

When the fiery liquid was pooling in her empty stomach, she became aware that nobody was talking. They were all looking at her.

'You know, I feel better already,' she said, angling a hard, accusing glance towards the silent figure who stood just to her right.

It had all been a mistake; she felt the anger like a tight fist in her chest. He has done this to me, she thought hating him as much as she had wanted him earlier.

'No, actually I do feel a bit hot and headachey now I think about it.'

A maternal hand was immediately clamped to her forehead. 'I don't think you have a temperature, but you can't be too careful.' Laura watched with a fixed smile as her daughter refilled her glass. 'Perhaps you should go and lie down…?'

'You know, I think I might.' Megan drained the glass and set it down with elaborate care on the table. 'Lovely to see you, Jean Paul. Catch up later, Uncle Mal,' she called out cheerily. She kissed her mother's cheek. 'I'm sure I'll feel better after a quick nap.'

She didn't say anything to Luc. She knew if she did that all the fury seething inside her would explode.

CHAPTER EIGHT

MEGAN didn't close the curtains. The moon had appeared and the leaded window was open. The soft breeze blowing through ruffled the heavy brocade curtains and cooled the warm, sticky night air.

She had slept in this room most of her life and she knew every creak and groan the ancient building could make. So when she heard a soft creak, Megan knew immediately that someone had stepped on the uneven floorboard just outside her door. That creaky floorboard had saved her from being caught reading under the covers on more than one occasion.

Mum, come to check up on me.

Sometimes, Megan decided, hiding your head under the bedclothes really was the only sensible thing to do. Before she did exactly that she twitched one of the drapes on her half-tester bed closed.

Lying there, eyes tightly closed she heard the door open. Though she strained her ears Megan couldn't hear footsteps on the polished oak floor. Pretending to be asleep when you knew someone was in the room watching you had seemed a lot easier when she was ten, she reflected as she did her best to keep her breathing even and relaxed.

The silent presence she sensed seemed to stand beside the bed for a very long time. It seemed as if hours had passed before she heard the door latch softly click closed. She exhaled a gusty sigh of relief.

'Thank goodness for that!' she breathed, rolling onto her back. With a soft grunt she pulled herself to her knees and drew back the curtain. It was as she pushed wayward strands of hair from her sticky, too-warm face with her forearm that Megan realised she wasn't alone.

Her midnight visitor was still there.

For a split second she just froze at the sight of the tall intruder standing with his broad shoulders set against the panelled oak door. The paralysis only lasted a fraction of a second before a massive rush of adrenaline was released into her bloodstream. Megan was out of the bed and standing there her body ramrod stiff.

Luc didn't think he had ever seen anyone radiate loathing quite so effectively as Megan did at that moment. So maybe convincing her he had always intended to come clean might not be easy…?

Easy? She's going to call you a lying bastard!

My God, had he messed up! It wasn't that he had *intended* for things to go that far before he told her the truth; not doing so had been one of the stupidest things he had ever done and he was totally prepared to admit it. The fact was, for the first time in his life he had let sexual hunger overrule common sense.

Megan watched as he lifted a hand to his forehead in a languid mocking salute. The colour seeped out of her skin, only emphasizing the sapphire shimmer of her eyes.

This was all a joke to him. God, but she had been such a fool! She had knocked back God knew how many decent men who liked her for a man who hadn't stopped lying to her from the moment they had met!

First Brian, now Luc—am I doomed to go through life being attracted to lowlife scumbags—? It was a deeply depressing thought, though, if she was honest, nothing she had felt for Brian in or out of bed resembled the passion that this man was capable of wakening in her. She had never hated Brian, or for that matter loved him. Whereas she hated Luc and…

'You lying, conniving rat!' she blasted.

I will not love him…I will not.

She stood there hating him, and hating even more the hot,

liquid tightening low in her pelvis and the inner knowledge that if he touched her she would be lost.

Her eyes slid of their own volition over his lean, muscular body. He was perfect, but it wasn't simply his physical perfection and startling male beauty that had her hooked, but the aura of raw sexuality that hung about him. She shivered. Everything he did, the slightest gesture, the way he turned his head, fascinated her.

'A touch hypocritical coming from someone who was pretending, very badly, to be asleep.'

He levered himself casually from the door frame.

'I thought you were my mother.'

'That makes it all right, then.'

She ground her teeth, knowing that if she opened her mouth without counting to twenty she would be shrieking like a fishwife in two seconds flat. She didn't want to risk getting incoherent or, worse, start bawling her head off. Megan wanted to tell him exactly what she thought of him.

'I'm assuming you're a little annoyed with me because I didn't tell you who I was—?'

'You're incredibly perceptive for a lying rat.'

'Do you think we could keep the rat references to the minimum? Can't stand the things.' 'He rubbed his forearm vigorously as he admitted with a grimace, 'They make my skin crawl.'

'*You* make my skin crawl,' she retorted childishly.

'No, I don't.'

The rippling sensation as all the muscles in her abdomen tightened wrenched a tiny grunt from her dry throat. His voice had a tactile quality that was like a caress.

Megan had never believed that violence solved anything, but as he stood there radiating total confidence she wondered if on this occasion it might not be the way to go. Even if it didn't solve anything, wiping that arrogant smirk off his face might make her feel better.

She took a deep, calming breath and told herself to rise above the provocation. Don't sink to his level.

'You like my skin, Megan.'

She started to shake her head until her eyes connected with Luc's. A slow, guilty flush spread over her face.

'Not the man inside it, I don't.' The skin, however, the smooth skin with its incredibly satiny texture, still, to her immense shame, exerted a strong tug to her senses.

His face tautened with anger.

'It wasn't my inner beauty you were interested in earlier.'

The awful thing was his mortifying observation could be equally true now. A fact hard to miss when no matter how hard she tried she couldn't stop her gaze straying to the point where the material of his shirt gaped, allowing a tormenting glimpse of flat brown belly.

He had been wearing the same shirt earlier. Megan had a horrible suspicion that she might have had something to do with that missing button.

Luc's jaw clenched as he bit back the oath that rose to his lips. 'If you stop sniping for thirty seconds I might be able to explain. I was going to tell you who I was, but—'

'But you thought it was a shame to waste the opportunity of a few more make-a-fool-of-Megan moments,' she inserted bitterly.

'I didn't want to make a fool of you, but you've got to admit you were phenomenally patronising when you rolled up at my place...'

'I was not patronising!' How could you be patronising when you were faced with a man who was, not only intimidatingly perfect and off-the-scale sexy, but quite obviously capable of delivering killer put-downs in his sleep?

'You wrote me off as the hired help, nice body but not much between the ears, the moment I walked in.'

'Your body isn't that good,' she lied. 'And I never thought you were stupid.' The intelligence in his eyes had been the first, well, maybe not *first* thing, but it had definitely been one of the first things she had noticed about him.

'Admit it,' he challenged. 'You're an intellectual snob of the worst kind.'

Her face got hot with anger at this totally unjust assessment. 'And you decided to teach me a lesson? That's why you came here pretending to be someone you're not.'

'Can you deny you needed a lesson? And I came here pretending to be me…'

'Being pedantic doesn't make you any less a total sleaze. Tell me, because I'm curious, what part of my lesson involved having sordid sex with me?'

'You seemed to enjoy sordid at the time,' he rebutted with brutal accuracy.

Megan flushed bright pink. 'Carry on thinking that if it makes you happy.' Without taking her eyes off his face, she reached for the bedside lamp; the lamp toppled and fell to the floor with a loud crash.

Megan didn't try and retrieve it. It wasn't as if the room wasn't bright enough—the moonlight streaming in through the window made the room as bright as day. The moon was so bright that she could see things she'd have been happier not seeing. Things like the shadow of body hair through his shirt…something that she was trying very hard *not* to see.

Besides that, this wasn't an occasion when moonlight was appropriate. Moonlight suggested romance and lovers.

'Are you going to pick that up?'

'No!' she snapped as he bent down. His head lifted. 'Leave it,' she snarled. 'You've got a cheek, I'll give you that. How dare you creep into my room? Get the hell out before I call for someone!'

Luc effected innocence. 'I thought we had a date?'

Her hands balled into fists. 'You must be joking!' she hissed. 'What you did was sick.'

'Stupid maybe,' came Luc's grim-faced admission.

Suddenly Megan wanted to cry. 'You're a cold, callous

bastard, and I'm so glad I entertained you.' Her feathery brows twitched. 'Do you generally have to pretend to be someone else to get a woman to sleep with you?'

Luc was starting to look exasperated. 'Look, I really regret what happened tonight.'

'Why—was I that bad?' In case he thought she was seeking reassurance, she added belligerently, 'You should know that I happen to know I was great.'

'You were great and then,' he drawled, 'you opened your mouth.' Even as he spoke an image flashed into his head of those soft, moist lips running over his naked skin. His eyes half closed, Luc's respiration started to come significantly faster as his body responded with painful urgency to the steamy image of Megan kneeling in front of him. It was so real that his long fingers flexed as he imagined himself winding them into the silky honey tresses as she knelt before him.

He touched the back of his hand to the beads of sweat along his upper lip and struggled to regain some control of his imagination.

Dear God, Luc, he told himself, you're acting like a teenager with his first rush of hormones!

'You seemed to think I was great too. In fact I seem to recall you saying you thought you were falling in love with me…?'

Megan froze. *'I did not!'*

'I could say *did too*, but not being five any more I won't. I'm prepared to give the benefit of the doubt…'

This man was quite simply unbelievable!

'The fact is I'm not happy with unquestioning adoration. I hate clingy women.'

'Do I look like I'm suffering from a case of adoration?'

'For crying out loud, woman!' he grated, an expression of seething frustration on his lean, strong-boned face. 'I came here to apologise but you make me so damned mad.'

His heavy-lidded glance slid downwards from the twin beacons of her blazing blue eyes.

At about the same moment Megan awakened to the uncomfortable fact she was standing there in a skimpy, short nightie. Her discomfort would have been ten times worse had she realised that the moonlight had rendered the fabric virtually transparent.

Luc was not similarly unaware and hadn't been since she had leapt from her bed. He was painfully aware of the outline of her slim, supple body. As much as he tried not to let them, his eyes were continually drawn to the gentle upward tilt of her rosy-tipped breasts and the strategic darker shadow at the apex of her long legs.

Megan resisted the urge to tug down the hem, and endured his scrutiny impassively. It isn't what you wear, it's the way you wear it—isn't that what Mum always says? Of course her mother, who bought sexy silk pyjamas half a dozen at a time from her favourite designer, would never have been caught wearing a cheap chain-store nightdress.

'Was it all a joke to you?' Megan asked.

His smoky gaze returned to her face; his manner was uncharacteristically distracted. 'Of course it wasn't a joke... I didn't expect tonight to go the way it did.'

'Well, I don't believe you,' she countered furiously. 'I think you planned everything. I think you're a cold, callous, manipulative snake.'

'Right, then, I don't suppose there's anything more to say.'

He's going now...say something. 'Fine, you know where the door is.'

Face like stone, Luc turned. 'See you around, Megan.'

'Not if I see you first,' she hissed.

The moment the door closed she crumbled.

CHAPTER NINE

MALCOLM, wearing silk pyjamas and a dressing gown, looked relieved when he saw Megan.

'I thought for a second you were your mother. I've been outside to have a couple of puffs on a cigar. You couldn't sleep either, huh?' He looked sympathetically at Megan, who was seated at the long scrubbed table in the cavernous kitchen.

Megan shook her head and nursed her mug of tea, which had gone cold while she'd sat there. She summoned up a weak smile and hoped her face had recovered from the worst of the tear damage. 'Bad night, Uncle Mal?'

'I never sleep in the country. Quite frankly I don't see how anyone does. It's so darned noisy,' he complained, dragging himself up a chair.

Despite her bleak frame of mind Megan was amused by his comment. As a country girl born and bred she couldn't let this comment go unchallenged.

'What about London traffic?' Even she, a sound sleeper—*normally*—found that hard to cope with sometimes.

'You can tune out traffic noises—wild animals making all sorts of unearthly noises through the entire night you cannot. Frankly, it gives me the creeps. Mind you, it's not as bad here as where Luc lives.' He gave a shudder. 'You have the sound of the sea to cope with there as well. God, the sound of the sea has to be the loneliest sound in the world.'

'That's really quite poetic, Uncle Mal.'

'Yes, I thought so too,' he agreed, looking pleased. 'Is there any tea in the pot?'

She shook her head. 'No, it's cold,' she said. 'I thought Luc said he lived in London.'

'Told you that, did he? Not like Luc to tell you anything beyond name, rank and serial number. He must have taken a shine to you.'

Megan laughed uncomfortably and said lightly. 'I doubt it.'

'No, the London place is a new thing. When he isn't traveling—a bit of a gypsy, our Luc is. You never know when he'll have the urge to take off. It's in his blood.'

Megan, who had heard the Land Rover revving up at three in the morning, lowered her gaze to the cold depths of her mug. She had seen the note on the hall stand addressed to her mother in a strong scrawl. It wouldn't be long before Malcolm discovered that Luc had taken off again...and good riddance!

'Normally he buries himself out in the wilds of the country, some place with a name I can't pronounce...Welsh. Not big on his fellow man, is Luc, but then,' he reflected, 'who can blame him under the circumstances?'

'What circumstances would those be?' Megan enquired.

'Said too much,' said Malcolm, looking alarmed.

'No, you've not said enough,' Megan corrected forcefully. She was sick to the back teeth with all this secrecy.

Malcolm sighed heavily. 'You're very like your mother sometimes,' he said. 'Now you must promise that what I tell you stays between us...?'

Megan gravely nodded.

'Luc had a successful business, engineering, he had a partner and, to cut a long story short, the partner had been draining the firm of funds for ages. The chap finally did a runner and left Luc to face the music.'

'Music...but I thought you said it was the partner...?'

'True, the only thing he had done wrong was trusting the wrong man. The police were very good, he said.'

'The police were involved!' she exclaimed.

'Sure, there was a full investigation and Luc was totally vindicated. It might have stopped there but one of the investors killed himself when he realised his life savings were down the toilet. Apparently the guy was pretty unstable to begin with, but when someone leaves a couple of kids and a pretty widow the press are not going to mention that. The press did a real job on Luc.'

The information was a lot for Megan to take in at once. 'Why don't I know about any of this?'

'It happened during your dad's last illness. Luc has changed a lot since then too; he doesn't look much like he did…short hair, sharp suits…people forget.'

'But Luc doesn't,' she said quietly.

'God, no!' exclaimed Malcolm. 'Luc isn't the forgiving and forgetting type.'

'Him and me both,' Megan gritted. No matter what had happened to Luc in the past, nothing made what he had done to her excusable.

'Relocation?' Megan repeated blankly. She had been finding it pretty hard to concentrate all day. It hadn't quite sunk in yet even though she had done the test twice—to be sure. It hadn't really been necessary—deep down she had already known, even before the little blue line had appeared.

There hadn't been symptoms as such, just a *feeling*. She had told herself that she was worrying unnecessarily, dates meant nothing, her cycle had always been pretty erratic.

She was still in denial. Of course she knew it happened, but not to her! The situation had been complicated by the fact that an old school friend was staying with her that week. Sophie was just about her best friend in the world, but confiding in her wasn't an option. Sophie had been married five years and had just completed her second lot of IVF treatment—how could you tell someone who was desperate to have a baby that you'd got pregnant accidentally?

'The quotes to bring the building in line with health and safety regulations have proved prohibitive.'

Megan struggled to concentrate on what her boss was saying.

'This a prime site for development and, apparently, it's economically more viable to sell and move out of the city.' He sighed. 'It's a charming part of the world, not far from a village called Underwood. I don't suppose you know the area...?'

'Actually I was brought up not far from there,' Megan admitted.

'Excellent. Well, you don't have to make any decision now, but we're very keen not to lose key staff like yourself. I think that once you've had a chance to examine the details, you'll find that the relocation package we're offering is generous—very generous indeed.'

For two days afterwards she pretended nothing had happened. On the third she took some of the leave she had accumulated and went home, it seemed the natural thing to do.

Her mother was away when Megan arrived at the house. The housekeeper, Elspeth, whom Megan had known since she was a child, explained that she had gone to Paris for a break.

'Do you know when she'll be back?' Megan asked.

'I couldn't say,' came the less-than-forthcoming response.

Another time Megan might have pressed the subject, but she had other things to think about. Maybe she was reading too much into the way Elspeth spoiled and fussed over her during the weekend, or maybe the older woman had inherited some intuitive powers from her Celtic forebears; either way Megan wasn't allowed to lift a finger. It was actually rather comforting to be fussed over.

The ancient walls of her childhood home had a strangely soothing effect upon her; the moment she walked through the door she experienced a strange sense of peace. Was it her condition that made her look at the beauty of her surroundings with different eyes? While she was walking in the woods one morning she came to a decision: she wanted her child to be brought up here where she had.

Laura returned on Sunday.

'You look incredible,' Megan told her as they took tea together in the pretty morning room. 'I really like your hair that way.'

'You don't think it's too…young…?'

'You are young, Mum.' Normally Megan would have picked up on her mother's tension immediately, but on this occasion she herself was distracted. Should she just come out with it, or would it be better to let her mother have a good night's sleep before she broke her news?

She took a deep breath…there was no good putting it off.

'Mum…'

'Megan, there's something I have to tell you…'

'Same here,' Megan said with a strained smile. 'After you…'

Laura got up and walked over to the low mullioned window. For the first time Megan registered her parent's unease. 'You know I went to Paris?'

Megan nodded. 'Yes?'

'I stayed with a friend.'

Her mother, her discomfort evident, was looking anywhere but at her. A knot of cold fear tightened in her stomach.

'That was nice,' she said, clenching and unclenching her white-knuckled hands as she worked up the courage to ask what she had to. 'You're not…ill, are you, Mum? If you are,' she added quickly, 'you mustn't panic. We can cope with whatever it is.'

When Laura turned and saw her daughter's face a grimace of self-recrimination crossed her own. The fear that lurked behind Megan's composed expression, she had seen before. At her lowest ebb, during her husband's illness and after his death, Megan had been a constant source of strength and comfort to them both, but sometimes Laura had seen that look…a shadow, really… It had made her feel guilty for relying so heavily on Megan.

'Gracious, no, I'm fine,' she assured Megan quickly.

Megan released a sigh of relief; nothing her mother had to say could be worse than what she had been imagining.

'Well, that's all right then. Who did you stay with? Anyone I know?'

Laura came and sat on the sofa beside her daughter. 'Jean Paul Legrand, you remember him…?'

'Tall, silver-haired, sexy French accent.' Laura gave a strained smile as her daughter reeled off the Frenchman's distinguishing characteristics. 'The dishy lawyer whose wife Dad went to college with.' Her brow creased. 'Didn't she die?'

'Yes, three years ago.'

'How is he?' She only had the vaguest recollections of how he'd looked that weekend a few weeks earlier. A few weeks…it felt like a lifetime ago.

'He's fine. Actually…' Laura sighed and caught Megan's hands. 'The thing is, darling, this isn't the first time I've stayed with Jean Paul and actually what I'm trying to tell you… Oh, my, this is very difficult.'

'Whatever it is it can't be as difficult as what I have to tell you,' Megan promised, her fingers tightening encouragingly around her mother's.

'Jean Paul has asked me to marry him and I've said yes.'

Megan's jaw dropped. Her mother getting remarried—it had been the last thing she had expected to hear. It was the last thing she had expected to happen! For the first time for a week she stopped thinking about her own situation.

'Marry…I didn't even know you were *seeing* him!' she exclaimed. Belatedly aware of her mother's anxious expression, she expelled a gusty sigh and pinned a suitably pleased smile on her face. 'But it's marvellous!' she cried, enfolding her mother in a bear-like hug.

Megan felt helpless when her mother began to cry.

'You mean that?'

Megan nodded. 'Of course I do.'

Laura released a shuddering sigh. 'I was so worried that you'd think I was being disloyal to your father's memory...I always said I would never get married again.' She lifted her head from her daughter's shoulder and accepted the tissue that Megan offered with a watery smile.

'Dad wouldn't have wanted you to be alone, Mum,' she said quietly. 'He was the last person who would have wanted you to live in the past.'

Laura sniffed and searched her daughter's face. 'You *really* don't mind?'

Megan shook her head. 'Of course I don't mind. I just want you to be happy. You love Jean Paul...?' It felt incredibly strange to be quizzing her mother on her romantic life. She noticed her mother looked as awkward as she felt.

'He's a lovely man—' Laura's self-conscious smile faded as her manner became solemn '—but he knows...' She shook her head. 'I made it quite clear to him that I wouldn't marry him if it upsets you.'

'So you want my blessing—? There's a bit of role reversal for you,' Megan teased, but her mother didn't smile.

'Yes, I do.'

'Then you have it.'

'Thank you, darling. It isn't the same as it was with your father...but, yes, I am very fond of him and he makes me laugh and feel young again.'

'Then I already love him,' Megan said fondly. 'Have you set a date?'

'We thought...well, there doesn't seem much point waiting under the circumstances.' She met her daughter's eyes and blushed. 'Neither of us are getting any younger...' she added quickly.

'So when…?'

'Next month.'

Megan let out a soundless whistle. 'Wow, you two don't let the grass grow, do you?' Despite her light-hearted tone Megan was beginning to be concerned that her mother was rushing into this.

'The thing is, Megan, Jean Paul's practice is in Paris. I'll be moving there. This place…it's such an enormous responsibility for you with your busy life.'

'Paris isn't very far, you mustn't worry about this place,' Megan said firmly. 'Actually, I might be around a lot more. The company is relocating to nine miles from here, of all places. So I'll be on hand to keep an eye on the old place.' Head tilted to one side, she scanned her mother's face. 'There's something else, isn't there?'

Laura nodded. 'Yes, there is.'

Megan's brows lifted. 'Well, go on,' she prompted, kicking off her shoes and drawing her knees up as she curled up cosily on the sofa. 'It can hardly be any more shocking than learning I'm about to have a new stepfather.'

Laura sighed and placed her interlinked hands on her lap. 'This is very embarrassing,' she groaned, closing her eyes. 'I'll just have to say it.'

'I wish you would,' Megan remarked. 'My imagination has gone into overdrive.'

'The thing is, Megan, I'm pregnant.'

A bubble of laughter escaped from Megan's throat. 'So what's really up?'

Her mother bit her lip and looked hurt. 'I'm not joking, Megan.'

Megan's jaw sagged. Her imagination, even in overdrive, had not produced this possible explanation.

'I know what you're going to say,' Laura rushed on, avoiding eye contact with her open-mouthed daughter. 'I can't be; I'm too old. That's what I said to the doctor when

he told me,' she admitted. 'But it seems I can be and I am...
actually I'm twelve weeks.'

'What does...does...Jean Paul say?' Does he know?'

'Of course he knows—it's not like I wouldn't tell him, is
it?' her mother rebuked gently and wondered at her daughter's guilt-stricken expression. 'Actually Jean Paul is being
marvellous about it, worried about my health, but everything's fine, I'm very fit. Marilyn couldn't have children,
you see, and this will be his first so he's very excited....'

Megan, her voice shaky, interrupted the flow. It still
didn't seem possible. 'You're *really* pregnant?'

Her mother nodded. 'Yes, I'm having a baby.'

Megan looked at her. 'Me too, Mum,' she said with a
high laugh that trembled on the brink of hysteria.

Laura's eyes widened. She scanned her daughter's face
and Megan nodded. 'It's true, I am.'

'Oh, my God!'

Suddenly mother and daughter were in one another's
arms, tears streaming down their cheeks.

Later when they were both cried out Laura turned to her
daughter. 'Now let's get practical. I'm assuming that Luc is
the father.'

'Why would you assume that?'

'Really, Megan! He couldn't take his eyes off you...I'm
assuming you had a falling out...?'

Megan nodded.

'You are going to tell him?'

'I don't know where he is...he's not in London.'

'Malcolm will know. I'll ask him.'

'No,' Megan replied. 'I'll ask.'

CHAPTER TEN

UNCLE MALCOLM had been reluctant to tell Megan where Luc was so she had been forced to tell him why she needed to see him.

'So you see I have to tell him, but,' she hastened to assure him, 'I'm not going to ask anything of him. It's my decision to have the baby...'

'Well, *obviously* you will have the baby.'

Megan inclined her head slightly in agreement. How obvious it had been had been something that still surprised her. Maybe there was a point with most women, even those like herself who had never even considered motherhood, when your body told you it was the right time.

Or maybe wanting to bear the child of the man you love has something to do with it...?

Megan gritted her teeth and ignored the sly voice in her head. 'And obviously he or she will be my responsibility and mine alone...'

'I expect Luc will want a quiet ceremony....'

Megan her cheeks still tinged with colour, looked at her uncle with exasperation. This she could do without! She couldn't afford to start thinking happy families even for one second...it was her duty to stay sane.

'Didn't you hear what I said? I want nothing from Luc.'

'I heard you, but that's plain silly. A child needs two parents.'

And a pregnant woman needs the loving father of her baby at her side. But that just isn't going to happen, Megan, so live with it.

'In a perfect world,' she agreed. 'However, lots of women

bring up children on their own.' And she was determined to make sure her child lacked for nothing. Even if Luc didn't want to take an active part in his child's life—a definite possibility—she would make sure that he or she felt loved and wanted.

'Lots of women don't have a choice,' her uncle rebutted.

'This argument sort of presupposes that Luc is going to ask me to marry him. Not very likely…we hardly know one another.' Which made the fact she had fallen in love with a man who was virtually a stranger all the more ludicrous.

'There's plenty of time to get to know someone after you're married.'

'You have a unique take on marriage, Uncle Malcolm.'

'And I think you'll find that Luc is actually quite traditional in a lot of ways.'

And he hates *clingy* women.

What man wasn't going to be horrified to discover that a woman he had had casual sex with once was carrying his child?

'Well, it doesn't really matter what Luc wants,' Megan, calm on the outside but a mass of conflicting emotions inside, told her uncle. 'Because I don't want to get married.' Not to a man who didn't love her, at any rate.

'You'll change your mind,' Malcolm predicted confidently before reflecting, 'I admit I didn't think so at the time, considering he had writer's block for the next six months, which threw the schedule all to hell, but it's turned out lucky under the circumstances that Grace wanted the divorce last year.' He appeared not to notice the spasm of shock that crossed his niece's face.

'Luc is married…? But—' She stopped abruptly, biting her lip so hard she broke the skin. But what, Megan? Why shouldn't Luc be married? Most men his age are or have been.

'*Was,*' Malcolm inserted with a worried look at her pale

face. 'He *was* married. They married when he was incredibly young, but they'd been apart for years. They'd just never bothered getting a divorce.'

Megan, who had a thousand questions, had pressed him for details, but Malcolm had infuriatingly clammed up, and advised her to ask Luc himself. And she was *really* going to do that! Of course you turned up on man's doorstep and said, Sorry, but I'm having your baby, and then asked him about the woman he actually loved.

Some things you didn't need to ask. She was no expert on marriage or divorce but Megan did know that people didn't *forget* to get a divorce. It wasn't the sort of thing that slipped your mind! It didn't take a genius to work out that couples who didn't legalise a split didn't do so because they hadn't given up yet. Luc and his wife had been leaving the door open for a reconciliation, and from what Malcolm had let slip it had been Luc's wife Grace who had finally closed that door.

Luc hadn't been able to work…*Grace*… Was this woman, whom Luc obviously still loved, as elegant and graceful as her name? Having discovered a previously untapped streak of masochism in her nature, Megan tortured herself on the trip to Wales imagining what the other woman looked like.

It was a long and tiring trip. She couldn't ring to let him know she was coming because Malcolm said he didn't have a phone at the cottage and always turned his mobile off when he was there. The cottage turned out to be not *quite* as isolated as her uncle had suggested. It hadn't been easy to find, though, and the last couple of miles proved the most challenging to her navigational skills.

After travelling a mile down a single track lane that was surrounded by high hedges that made it impossible to see anything, being suddenly confronted with an incredible view of the stormy sea took Megan's breath away. She stopped the car and wound down the window to take it all in. The salty tang filled her lungs as she gazed at the scene: white-crested waves crashing onto the pebbly foreshore.

With a sigh Megan turned off the ignition; there was no point putting off the inevitable.

Cautiously—the track was full of potholes—she negotiated the path down the steep slope that led to the solitary habitation. The cottage, set on a rocky outcrop of higher ground, was situated just above the rocky seashore. The high tide lapped up against a low wall, which appeared to be the only defence against the sea. The low whitewashed building was not large, but its walls looked sturdy enough to withstand the worst the harsh elements could throw at it. It looked old enough to have been doing just that for a couple of hundred years at least.

A mud-spattered four-wheel drive Megan immediately recognised stood on a small level area in front of the cheerily red-painted front door.

Megan turned off the engine and pressed her hand flat to her chest. When your heart felt as if it were trying to escape from your chest it probably was not a good time to recall stories about apparently healthy people who dropped dead from undiagnosed heart complaints.

Maybe I should rethink this plan…? Maybe I should drop it altogether.

Calm down, Megan, you know exactly what you're going to say. 'Just a courtesy call—I'm going to have your baby.'

Oh, dear…! Considering she had been working on the intro for the last three hundred miles, that could do with some work.

She felt physically sick as she lifted the door knocker and let it fall. When nobody replied she walked around the building peering in the windows. There was no evidence of life. Was this a sign? Was some higher authority telling her she should go home? There did seem something awfully confrontational about rolling up on a man's doorstep and telling him you were carrying his child.

Megan wasn't a confrontational person by nature.

Sure, a letter was impersonal, but was impersonal such a bad idea in this instance? The impersonal method actually had a lot to recommend it—a letter was much neater and there would be much less opportunity for her to make a total fool of herself and do something embarrassing like burst into tears.

After a brief struggle with herself, Megan decided to give it another half-hour and then return to the village she had passed through a few miles back and see if they had a room for the night. Even if she didn't see Luc she was in no condition to drive back home tonight.

Sitting in the car, she felt stiff and cold; within five minutes she lost all feeling in her extremities. Rubbing her hands together, she turned on the engine. The warmth blasted out by the heater going full throttle and the music on the radio had a predictably soporific effect.

Megan was gently dozing off when the door of the car was wrenched open without warning. It stayed open as, hands pressed on the roof, Luc bent down until he was on eye level with Megan. She thought she had committed every detail, every impossibly symmetrical detail of his face to memory, but now his dark, hard-edged face was within inches of hers she realised that he was far, *far* more beautiful in the flesh.

Thinking about flesh had not been a good move. Her stomach muscles quivered and shifted as images crowded in her head of smooth, sleek skin sheathing tight hard muscles. She had read that pregnancy could kill a girl's libido stone-dead…it turned out she wasn't one of this number!

'It's a very nice place you have here.' Did those terminally stupid words come out of my mouth? This really wasn't how this scene had played in her head.

'And you just happened to be passing?'

His deadly irony brought a flush to Megan's pale cheeks.

'I would have phoned.'

Luc lifted a hand to his dark, wind-ruffled hair. It curled onto his neck. It didn't look to Megan as though it had been cut since she saw him last. 'I don't use a phone for a reason...I don't like to be disturbed by uninvited guests when I'm working.'

She let her eyes slide over his olive-green waterproof jacket that was open at the neck to reveal a black sweater. Her examination moved lower, over his long legs encased in moleskins, and ended on his walking boots. He looked lean and fit, leaner maybe than the last time she had seen him...

She watched, unwillingly riveted as he lifted a hand to his wind-ruffled hair. His face, too, seemed thinner, with the strong bones and angles seeming more pronounced. His eyes were the same, though...an illicit little shiver ran down her spine as she diverted her gaze to a point over his shoulder.

'Are you working now?'

'I'm a writer. Writers are always working,' Luc lied calmly. He hadn't written a word since he'd got down here. 'For me a walk along the beach usually focuses my thoughts nicely.' Recently they had only been on Megan's eyes, her smell, her sweet softness... Of course this obsession would pass. The irresponsible part of him suggested he enjoyed it while it lasted. But it was easier to ignore that irresponsible voice when she was three hundred miles away.

Everyone, he told himself, determinedly ignoring the ache in his groin, knew that recognising you had a problem was part of the cure.

And Luc had recognised he had a problem with Megan from day one.

'Inspiration strikes when you're least expecting it.'

Like love, Megan thought, and gave a disbelieving sniff. 'What do you do, carry a notebook and jot things down? No wonder you've got so many friends,' she muttered under her breath.

Did he ever invite any of those selected few, and she was

thinking female here, to this place? Did they spend weekends cosily shut away from the world together? What was
there to do but walk on the beach and make love? Her hands
clenched as she imagined those steamy lovers' trysts.

'No need for notes; I have an excellent memory.'

His excellent memory was at that moment recalling the
huskiness of her voice as she had called his name and said
she'd never have enough of what he was doing to her. Never
have enough of him, and begged him… He drew a deep
breath and stopped thinking about the liquid heat of her tight
around him.

He was obviously an individual who was drawn to un-
suitable women; first Grace, and now Megan. Was it ge-
netic…?

A man had to learn by his mistakes and Luc had made
this mistake once before. At least last time he'd had extreme
youth and rampant hormones to blame. This time around he
was old enough and bruised enough by life to be able to
know that instant attraction and great sex were not enough.
There had to be more.

What that *more* was he had yet to figure out.

A shocking idea was forming in Megan's head. My God,
had she been part of his research for his latest book? The
idea made her feel physically sick. 'Well, if I ever discover
someone who resembles me in one of your books I'll sue,'
she told him fiercely.

'I thought you didn't read my stuff.'

Megan shrugged at the taunt and watched as Luc, one
hand braced at the base of his spine, straightened up and
rotated his shoulders, as if the position he'd been hunched
in had put a few kinks in his spine.

'Only when my train is late,' she retorted, grabbing her
bag off the passenger seat and preparing to make best use
of the fact he wasn't guarding her exit.

'Don't even think about getting out,' he growled.

Megan stopped dead and lifted her glance to his. Luc's

expression held more hostility than she would have thought possible.

He hates me… She swallowed past the emotional thickening in her throat and lifted her chin. So she hadn't expected him to open the champagne, but neither had she expected this level of antagonism.

'I'm going to do more than that,' she promised him, flashing a smile that ached with insincerity.

Not a single muscle moved in his stony expression. 'Just turn the car around and go back home, Megan.' He ran a hand over his jaw, his attitude now more weary than hostile. 'We have nothing to say.'

That's all he knows! 'My God, you're rude!'

He blinked as he looked into those stunning blue eyes that shone with disgusted condemnation. 'I'm the rude one?' he bit back. 'That's rich—you're the one who just turns up on my doorstep uninvited. If you want to take up where we left off you can forget it…I like to make the first move.' And he would if he let her within ten feet of him; along with common sense, the self-control he was so proud of deserted him around this woman.

Making the first move…now *that* she remembered. Actually she remembered everything and it made it hard for her to think this close to him.

Luc's brows knitted in a dark frown as he looked at her.

'Look, we always seem to be yelling at each other! Megan said, noticing just how tired she was feeling.

'You were the only one yelling.'

'I had reason to yell. You lied and cheated your way into my life. Looked down your nose at my family and friends and then accused me of falling in love with you!' A flush of mortification washed over her skin as she recalled their parting.

She might have been able to forgive him if she hadn't realised that his diagnosis had been spot on. She had been in love with him.

'Anyway you had plenty to say then,' she reminded him grimly. 'And now it's my turn, and I didn't drive all this way to go back without saying it. And if you think for one second that I'm going to turn around just because you say so, then you're wrong.'

She was aware that Luc was watching her as she got out of the car. His silent scrutiny was partially responsible for her inelegant exit; the rest was down to the intense exhaustion that had hit her like a brick wall. Her brain felt even less nimble than her feet, which was not a good thing considering the importance of what she had come here to tell him.

She lost her balance and almost fell as she stepped away from the car. Saving herself without making use of the steadying hand Luc shot out, Megan tilted her gaze up to his and saw his lips twist in a wry smile as his hand dropped to his side.

He didn't say anything; he didn't do anything, except look enigmatic and gorgeous enough to make the average woman weep.

She took a deep breath.

'I have been driving for hours; my back hurts.' She grimaced as she pressed her hand to the base of her spine. 'I need a cup of tea and I need a bathroom, the latter fairly urgently.'

'I suppose you'd better come in.'

The grudging invitation brought a twisted smile to Megan's pale lips. 'How can I resist when you ask so nicely?' Not resisting Luc was what had got her in this position to begin with.

CHAPTER ELEVEN

MEGAN followed Luc inside the cottage, her low-heeled shoes clicking on the flagged floor. The interior layout was a surprise to Megan. The internal dividing walls were gone, creating one large open-plan living area that used up the entire ground-floor space. The original flagged floor had been retained, as had the vast inglenook, but the modern kitchen appliances and stylish Swedish wood burner were very sleek and state-of-the-art.

The heat being thrown out by the wood burner made Megan reach for the scarf that was wrapped around her throat.

'Bathroom…?'

'Up there,' he said, a beat behind.

Megan followed the direction of his nod and walked towards the wrought-iron spiral staircase. It wasn't until she reached the upper floor that she realised that the stairs opened directly into a room. The faint scent of the male fragrance Luc used hung in the air; it made her nostrils flare and sensitive stomach muscles tighten.

So this, she thought, releasing a long sigh, was Luc's bedroom, her pulse rate suddenly going through the roof.

Luc's bedroom was a place she had dreamed about a lot lately but she hadn't expected to find herself there. Furnished in a minimal style she recognised immediately from downstairs. Again the internal walls had been knocked out to make a space that was almost as large as the room below. The roof though was open to the rafters and light flooded in through the window.

Either Luc had just had a spring-clean or he was very neat; there wasn't a dirty sock or crumpled shirt in sight. In fact there was nothing much in sight beyond a couple of vibrant rugs on the oiled oak floor, a chair, a set of bookshelves and a bed—a large bed.

Megan swallowed. A *very* large bed, she thought, staring at the smooth sheets and simple throw.

She was looking around for the bathroom when she saw the wall.

'Oh, my God!'

Up to this point her back had been turned to it, but now she could see that the wall was covered, *entirely* covered from ceiling to floor in photos. Black-and-white prints that overlaid each other in a gigantic collage.

Even to her uneducated eye it was obvious that she wasn't looking at snapshots. The subject matter was diverse. They ranged from stormy seascapes and wild mountain scenery to pictures of old wrinkled men sitting around a chessboard, pipes in hands, and women with babies on their backs and water-pots on their heads, to children with even older faces searching rubbish dumps for food.

Faces frozen in time or starkly beautiful places, the pictures all had a quality, not just great lighting or inspired subject matter, but an indefinable *something* that made the observer stand and stare. Megan did. Despite the urgency of her errand she stood for a long time just looking.

If Luc had taken these himself he was not only very well travelled, but incredibly talented.

She finally managed to tear herself away, her mind still filled with the images she had seen and Megan had to open several doors before discovering the bathroom. Was Luc's mind as organised as his storage space? Unlike his bedroom, the bathroom was neither spartan nor rustic.

Megan looked around curiously and liked what she saw. It was tiled in pale cream stone tiles, which reflected the light flooding in through the roof windows. The bath, a freestanding decadent French slipper job that could have held half a football team. The bathroom in her flat could have fitted into the state-of-the-art shower cubicle.

'So this hasn't started well,' she admitted to her reflection in the mirror. 'That means things can only get better.' With the best will in the world Megan couldn't inject an authentic note of optimism into her voice.

When she went back downstairs Luc was in the kitchen area at the opposite end of the room. He had taken off his outdoor clothes, including the heavy sweater he had been wearing. He stood there in the dark moleskins that clung to the long line of his well-developed thighs. The rolled up sleeves of his pale blue shirt revealed the subtle sinewed strength of his forearms and the even tone of his dark skin.

Would there ever come a day when she would be able to look at him and not be paralysed with lust? Megan forced herself to release the air trapped in her tight chest.

He didn't look up even though he must have heard her come down.

Perhaps he was hoping that she'd go away if he pretended she wasn't there?

She watched as, very much at home in the kitchen, he rattled around in a competent manner in a cupboard, then walked over to a sink and filled a kettle. Even doing something mundane he was always a pleasure to watch and she was glad of anything that delayed the moment she would have to reveal why she was here.

She shifted her weight from one foot to the other and her elbow caught against the wall. She winced as pain shot up her arm. She rubbed it and realised that Luc was watching her.

'Find what you needed?'

She nodded and he returned to his task. 'Did you take the photos upstairs?' She did feel a need to break the lengthening silence, but she was also genuinely curious.

'Yes, did you like them?'

She nodded and then realised he wasn't looking at her.

'Very much, you're very talented.' Multi-talented, it would seem. 'Did you train?' He could easily have made his living out of them. It must have been hard to make the choice between writing and becoming a professional photographer.

'No, I've always taken photos. When I was making a living doing something that bored me rigid it was the only thing that kept me sane.'

'Why were you doing it if you hated it?'

Luc, who was taking a carton of milk from the big American-style fridge, had his back to her.

'I had my own business, and I was doing it for the same reason most people do jobs they don't like.' He turned, his mocking gaze sweeping across her face. 'Money.'

'And did you make a lot?'

'Yes, I made a lot of money.' His long, curling lashes lifted from the slashing curve of his cheekbones. 'And then,' he added, pinning her with a mocking stare, 'I lost it.' He had sold everything he had to pay off the creditors and clients that his partner had stolen from. 'All of it and then some.'

Aware that she wasn't supposed to know about his business, she said, 'That must have been terrible.'

'I thought so at the time.'

'I don't think I could do that,' she mused.

'Do what? Lose money?'

'Do something I hated just for money.' The look she directed towards him was tinged with reproach. 'Especially if I was as talented as you are.' With no talent for anything artistic, she had always envied people who were.

His expressive mouth twisted in a derisive smile. 'You could, believe me you could. Job satisfaction is nice, but so,' he added drily, 'is eating. I like to eat, most people do, and relatively few have the luxury of being able to pick and choose what they do. It's easy to turn up your aristocratic little nose when you've never had to worry about money. You've always had the cushion of Daddy's millions.'

A mortified flush travelled over Megan's fair skin. She swallowed hard. His scalding derision was well deserved. She was deeply ashamed that she had sounded like a spoilt little rich girl.

Actually her strict parents had never overindulged her. They had gone out of their way to teach her the value of money, but Luc was right, she reflected with a repentant shake of her head—she didn't know what it was to worry about money. Compared to many, her life had been easy.

'You're right, that was a really stupid thing to say.' She heaved a sigh. How many women who had found themselves in her present situation had not had the luxury of choice?

It was a sobering thought. Sadly money did make a difference. 'I do appreciate that I'm incredibly lucky, you know,' she told him huskily.

The cynical sneer faded from Luc's face as he stood there for a moment, recognising the unmistakable glow of genuine penitence shining in her blue eyes. The line above the bridge of his masterful nose deepened.

Megan got the impression that for some reason her response had surprised him...disappointed him even...as though he *wanted* her to do something he could disapprove of. She almost instantly dismissed this fanciful idea.

'The photos really are very good, you know. Have you ever though of exhibiting any?' she wanted to know.

'Have you been talking to Malcolm?'

Megan froze guiltily. 'No, yes...well, he didn't want to tell me you were here. Why do you ask?'

'Oh, I thought maybe he had sent you here as his advocate.'

She shook her head. Her instincts told her to drop the subject but her curiosity wouldn't let her. 'Advocate for what?' she asked.

'Oh...' he shrugged carelessly... 'his latest money-making

project. Ever since Malcolm saw my gallery upstairs he's been nagging me to publish a book of them.'

'And you don't want to?' It sounded like a great idea to her. 'If Uncle Malcolm says there's a market for that sort of thing, I'm sure he's right,' she ventured tentatively.

Her earnest defence of her uncle brought an amused, 'Are you *sure* he hasn't got to you?'

'No, he hasn't, but if he had I'd have told him the best way to get you to agree was to let you think it was your brilliant idea to begin with.'

He looked at her, startled for a moment, then the stern lines of his face melted into a grin.

Megan grinned back. 'I did a psychology module in my first year at uni,' she explained.

Her laughing eyes meshed with his, the moment of harmony didn't last long. At almost the exact moment that Megan recognised the atmosphere had changed, that the air between them throbbed with unspoken and dangerous things, Luc stopped laughing. Megan touched her tongue to the perspiration beading her upper lip and the pupils of Luc's eyes dramatically dilated. She saw him swallow before his dark head angled away from her.

'Tea or a beer?' he asked, not looking up.

'Tea.' If he could act as though nothing had happened so could she. Maybe she was the one who had started reading sex into everything because she was obsessed—not Luc.

'Do you mind if I sit down?' She didn't wait for his response; if she didn't sit down soon she would fall. Her knees were shaking. She presumed it was a reaction to the confrontation—she hated confrontations. It couldn't be good for the baby for her to feel this terrible. In an unconsciously protective gesture her hands went to her still-flat belly.

She sank into the soft chair and tried to think calm thoughts…it was an ambitious plan. Her brain was firing off questions one after the other in rapid succession; there was no let-up from the anxiety-inducing bombardment. How would Luc react? Was he going to be angry? Shocked, obviously—heaven knew she had been! Was he even going to believe her?

When Luc approached, mugs of tea in hand, Megan saw his bare feet. Her stomach muscles fluttered. How could she, how could *anybody* find bare feet erotic? Now hands, yes. Luc had the most beautiful hands, expressive hands with long, sensitive fingers... This time the tightening of her stomach muscles was vicious.

Catching the direction of her fixed gaze, Luc offered a curt explanation of, 'Under-floor heating,' before he nudged an open laptop to one side and set a mug of hot tea on the rustic oak coffee table.

Megan ran her fingers across the oiled surface of the wood. The cottage was filled with natural materials and textures and it was all very tactile and sensual. But nothing she had seen in the cottage made her want to reach out and touch more than the man who took a seat opposite her.

Megan nodded her thanks as her fingers closed around the hot, steaming mug, and pretended she was looking at the flickering images of the screen saver while she was actually greedily observing him fold his long length with fluid grace into a Kelim-covered sofa opposite her. Something in her stomach twisted painfully as she looked at him.

The feeling didn't go away when she stopped looking.

Luc glanced at his watch.

The pointed gesture brought a resentful sparkle to her eyes. This was about the single most momentous moment in her life and he didn't even bother disguising he couldn't wait to see the back of her. Deep down she knew it was irrational to feel angry. Luc didn't have the faintest idea why she was here—not that anything excused this boorish display of bad manners.

'I'm so sorry if I'm keeping you from something more important,' she drawled sarcastically.

'Only a couple of thousand words.' Luc, who hadn't been

able to write a word since he'd arrived at the cottage, lied. He leaned forward and rested his chin on the platform of his interlocked fingers.

Megan shivered as his silvered appraisal moved over her.

'You've lost weight,' he judged with a disapproving frown.

'A little,' she admitted.

'It doesn't suit you.'

Megan let the brutal observation pass; she recognised a perfect opening when she heard it. Then again, he wasn't in the best of moods—perhaps she should wait. Wait until when you give birth…? Tell him, Megan, *now…now…*the voice in her head prompted urgently.

As she opened her mouth her heart was beating so fast she could hardly breathe.

'Don't worry, I'll be putting the pounds on again soon,' she said, fixing her eyes firmly on her hands clasped neatly in her lap.

There was a silence, which got longer until, frustrated to the point of screaming, Megan lifted her gaze to his.

'You were supposed to ask *why*!'

'Why what?'

'Why will I be putting on weight…?' she prompted.

A flicker of amusement momentarily lightened the wariness in his eyes. 'Why will you be putting on weight, Megan?' he asked obligingly.

'I will be putting on weight because that's what people do when they're pregnant, which I am…pregnant, that is.'

There, it was out! She ought to be feeling a sense of release, but what she was actually feeling was sick…very sick. She pressed a hand to her mouth and waited, her eyes half closed, for the waves of nausea to pass.

When the imminent danger of throwing up had passed, she swallowed and opened her anxious eyes. Luc hadn't moved a muscle since she had blurted out her news. She gave a frustrated sigh. Whatever he was feeling, she wasn't going to see it here—a granite rock face would have been easier to read than those strong symmetrical contours. It was actually his total *lack* of response, his eerie stillness, that revealed he had even heard what she had said.

'With your baby...obviously.' She coloured. Maybe it wasn't *obvious* at all to him?

It was possible that he thought she acted with equal wanton abandon with every man that took her fancy...

On the brink of making a disastrous confession, Megan bit her tongue. Luc didn't need to hear how special he was, and the fact that she had never felt that way with any other man was something that ought to be kept on a need-to-know basis, and he *definitely* didn't need to know!

'Don't worry, I'm not here to make a scene,' she told him, gruffly earnest. 'I just thought that you had the right to know. And,' she added, 'it's not the sort of thing that's easy to say in a letter. Actually it's not the sort of thing that's easy to say full stop,' she added in a dry undertone. Belatedly she realised this comment might have come over as a little light on empathy. 'Or hear,' she tacked on generously.

Luc's vibrant complexion had acquired a grey tinge as he lost the last shred of his habitual cool. She'd been prepared for shaken, but Megan got seriously alarmed when he suddenly buried his face in his hands. His classical profile was hidden from her view, but she could hear the laboured sound of his breathing from where she was sitting.

After a few moments his head lifted and she was relieved to see his colour was improved. 'A *baby*...?'

She nodded, sympathetic to his traumatised condition.

He shook his head from side to side in the hope the action might kick-start his numb brain.

'So you weren't taking the pill...?' He saw the pain flare in her eyes and thought, Good move Luc, let her think you're blaming her, you insensitive bastard.

'I'm afraid I didn't think...I should...'

'Neither of us thought, Megan.' His expressionless voice cut into her disjointed stream of self-recriminations.

Megan lapsed into unhappy silence. Through the mesh of her lashes she watched his chest lift as he sucked in a deep breath.

'I'm sorry, you must be—'

'I'm not asking for anything from you,' she interrupted quickly. She saw some emotion, indefinable but strong, flare briefly in his eyes before she ploughed heavily on. 'I appreciate this is my responsibility. Of course, if you want to have some input, that is fine.'

CHAPTER TWELVE

'INPUT…' Luc repeated, looking at Megan as though she had run mad.

She exhaled a small gusty sigh of relief as she managed to wrench her fascinated eyes from the muscle in his lean cheek that was clenching and unclenching. 'And if you don't that's equally fine,' she told him with an upbeat smile. 'There's no pressure.'

'Are you trying to be funny?'

'I'm trying to be positive,' she rebutted. Considering she was attempting to make this easy for him, he didn't seem wildly appreciative.

His narrowed eyes scanned her face. 'So you've decided to have this baby.'

'You sound surprised?'

His brows lifted. 'Well, what about your career?'

'What about my career?' Angrily, she pretended not to see where he was going with this.

'I thought that was the most important thing in your life. The thing you're prepared to sacrifice a personal life for.'

'It is part of my life, and it is important, but my priorities have changed…' Her expression grew defensive. 'I'm allowed to change my mind.'

'It could change again…?'

Megan's heart gave a sickening thud. This was what she had been dreading him suggesting. She shook her head and ran her tongue over her dry lips. 'No, I've thought this thing through quite carefully,' she insisted. 'I'm sorry,' she said, feeling the prickle of hot tears behind her eyelids. 'I can see how you'd like this to go away, but I want this baby.'

An expression of revulsion crossed his face. 'Are you suggesting I would pressure you into having a termination?'

As this was exactly what she had assumed he was talking about, she just stared back at him mutely. His white-lipped fury gave lie to her assumption that he was taking this reasonably calmly under the circumstances.

Luc wasn't calm, unless you considered volcanoes about to erupt calm!

'I misunderstood,' she admitted with a shrug. Misunderstanding or not, there was a point that needed making here. 'Accidental or not, you're the baby's father… I can't prove it, of course—'

'For God's sake, woman, of course it's my baby. Do you think I imagine you make a habit of having unprotected sex any more than I do?' he demanded impatiently. The furrow between his brows deepened as their eyes locked. 'My God,' he breathed. 'You did think that, didn't you?'

Megan shook her head, then nodded, then grabbed two handfuls of hair and grimaced as she rocked forward and back again. 'I don't know what I thought,' she admitted huskily.

The anger faded from Luc's face as he looked at the dejected, dispirited set of her hunched shoulders. 'It must have been a confusing few weeks for you. It might make things a little easier to have someone to talk this out with…?'

The soft suggestion brought her head up with a snap. 'Get any idea I came here to ask your advice right out of your head. I already know what I'm going to do,' she ground out.

'So basically what you're saying is you're going to do exactly what you want to, no matter what I say.' His eyes, like molten silver, locked onto hers.

'In a nutshell.'

Luc took a deep sustaining breath and told himself he didn't have the right to be angry. What else could she have said? He'd backed her into a corner.

He even agreed with her, in the abstract, *her* body…*her*

baby…*her* decision, but this wasn't an abstract baby. This wasn't just *any* baby. It was *his* baby… A few minutes ago he'd been aghast to hear what she had come to tell him, with bewildering speed his attitude had undergone a dramatic change. It amazed Luc how the idea of having a child could grow on a man.

'So if you've thought this out, tell me, how are you going to cope with a baby and a demanding job?'

'As luck would have it the firm I work for is relocating to a site nine miles from home so I'm going back,' she explained. 'It's a good place to bring up a child. I should know; I was brought up there.'

'And you're expecting your mother to bring up your child for you… Have you considered that having a young baby foisted on her at her age might not be what she wants? What's so funny?' he wanted to know when her lips twitched.

Megan shook her head, she judged that he had had enough shocks for one day. Besides, this wasn't her news to share. 'Actually,' she explained, 'Mum is moving to Paris.'

The quiver of laughter in her voice made his strong features clench in disapproval. 'Planning to give birth at your desk and be back at it the next day?'

'I'm planning on taking maternity leave,' she contradicted, 'and afterwards…' her shoulders lifted '…the firm has no problem with job-sharing.' She'd been thinking on the way down that this might be the way to go. The balance between work and home was going to be hard to get right, but she was determined to strike a balance that she could live with.

Luc gave a thin smile, he didn't bother to hide his scepticism as he snorted, '*Job-sharing!* Is the real Megan in there—?' He stretched his hand out, intending to touch the side of her head.

Megan, who knew exactly what the casual contact would

do to her, flinched away before he made contact. She saw his jaw tighten and repressed a groan. Well, she told herself, if he thought she couldn't bear to have him touch her, so much the better. If he knew how much she craved his touch it would only complicate things even more—it wouldn't do her pride much good either.

'What do you mean?' As if she didn't know.

'Well, you have to admit job-sharing doesn't sound like you.'

'You don't know me.' *Neither do I, these days.* 'And why do you assume that I'm going to be a disaster as a mother?' she asked sharply. She might not have felt this angry if his dig hadn't magnified her own fear that she would be inadequate for the daunting task of parenting.

'Why do you assume that I'd be relieved to offload my responsibilities to this baby?' he countered.

Protesting that it wasn't the same thing at all would have laid her open to a legitimate accusation of sexism. Instead Megan shook her head and insisted, 'I didn't.' Then added weakly, 'Not exactly.'

'I just don't believe you sometimes. You think I'd let my child grow up not knowing who the hell I was!'

He shook his dark head and she thought, God, he's *furious.*

'As for all that rubbish about you being responsible, like they say it takes two…and I was most *definitely* there. Or had you forgotten?'

His response was the first indication she had had so far that he wanted anything to do with the baby and Megan wasn't sure how she felt about it. What was he talking about anyway? Gifts and cards on birthdays and Christmas? Every other weekend and alternate summer holidays?

The image of a future where Luc turned up with his latest girlfriend in tow to take their child to the zoo filled her with horror.

'I wish I could forget!'

A raw silence fell between them.

A cautious light entered her eyes as she looked across at him from under the protective shade of her lashes. She was almost sure he didn't even know that he was grinding one clenched fist into the other open palm. It was very much the action of someone who was struggling to suppress strong emotions. She could see every sinew, every taut muscle of his lean body screaming with tension.

'I'm going to be a father.' He said it as it had just begun to sink in.

There was a blank look of incomprehension on his lean, devastatingly handsome features in the moment before he leapt to his feet in one lithe motion.

'Luc…?' He appeared not to hear her tentative voice as, with one fist clenched to his forehead in an attitude of deep thought, the other thrust in the pocket of his snug-fitting trousers, he began to pace from one end of the room to the other.

It was impossible, even in her present distraught frame of mind, not to look at him and experience a shivery frisson of sensation in the pit of her stomach while hearing the words *lithe* and *luscious* in her head.

'If you need time to think about this, I understand…' Coming here had been a mistake, a major mistake.

'Shut up, I'm thinking.'

Megan's eyes narrowed at his tone. 'I'm being understanding,' she told him wrathfully.

He looked over his shoulder and for a moment the intensity of his expression melted into a delicious grin. 'Be understanding quietly, *chérie*,' he instructed, pressing a finger to his lips.

Even without the grin the endearment would have got to her; with it she melted like butter on a hot knife.

He continued to pace for a few more minutes before moving back to the sofa. He sat on the edge, his body curving towards her so that their knees were almost touching. His body language created an illusion of intimacy that made it difficult for Megan to think straight. She had a horrible notion that her feelings were written in letters a mile high across her forehead as she gazed back at him, but she couldn't do a thing about it.

'I want…' he studied her face for a moment before his sensual lips slowly curled upwards into a self-derisive smile while she tensed her body, almost quivering with anticipation '…*Input*.'

Colour flooded Megan's pale face; the embarrassment and anticlimax was intense.

'Megan…?'

Megan blinked before arranging her features into something approaching composure. Just what made you think he was going to say I want you? That was the last time she went into fantasy mode. The fact was if Luc had wanted her, he could have had her.

'Fine.'

His eyes narrowed warily. 'You don't sound fine.'

'Are you going to dissect every inflection in my voice?' she demanded spikily.

He shrugged, and *almost* grinned. 'Point taken.' He leaned back into the squashy cushions of the sofa and, hands linked behind his head, looked at the ceiling.

What's he thinking? she wondered. No more wild guesses for her. She didn't have to wait long to find out.

'Do you actually think it is such a good idea?'

He rubbed his scalp vigorously with his long fingers, causing his dark hair to stick up in sexy tufts on the crown. Megan, her expression abstracted, was watching as he smoothed down the dark strands of glossy hair. She remembered sinking her fingers into that silky dark thatch and drawing his head down to hers.

'Do I think what is a good idea?'

'You moving back home…'

This casual comment focused her attention.

She smiled narrowly and sucked in her breath. 'Naturally

your opinion means just so much to me…' Luc grimaced, rolled his eyes towards the ceiling, before folding his arms across his chest in an attitude of long-suffering patience. The action incensed her further. 'But I find myself thinking just what the hell has it got to do with you? I'm having a baby—that doesn't mean I'm going to have anyone treating me like one!'

'Finished?'

Megan sniffed and refused to let him see how close to tears she was.

'I have absolutely no desire to pull your strings…' Just pick you up and carry you to my bed. 'Besides, I'd have to be mad to even try—you're about as malleable as a steel bar.' But very much softer to hold.

Not the most flattering comparison she had ever heard, but she was glad he realised she wasn't a pushover.

'Can I finish saying something without you jumping down my throat?'

Megan gave a curt nod of her head. 'I'll listen.'

'I can see why you might want to move back home at the moment, familiar surroundings…people willing to wait on you hand and foot…'

'I'll forget the people-willing-to-wait stuff.' He obviously had no idea about the staffing levels on the estate. 'But what's wrong about wanting to be in familiar surroundings?' she challenged.

'They're not *your* surroundings.'

She frowned and he looked exasperated. 'I know it will be yours one day, but right now it's your mother's home, and she doesn't look like she's going to vacate the position of lady of the manor any time soon to me. You can't run back to Mummy every time the going gets tough, Megan.'

'She won't be there.'

'You know what I mean. You need your own home, Megan. You need to start as you mean to go on.'

'The estate is my home.'

'It's your mother's home.

She shook her head. 'Underwood doesn't belong to my mum.'

Luc looked puzzled. 'Then who does it belong to?'

'It's mine. I thought you knew.'

She saw the shock register on his face. '*You* own the estate?'

Megan nodded.

She watched him as the information sank in. 'Does that mean you're filthy rich?'

'Why, Luc? Wishing you hadn't chucked me out of your bed?' she taunted.

Luc inhaled sharply. 'I didn't do that, Megan, and you know it. I couldn't have even if I wanted to,' he commented with a self-derisive grimace. 'For the simple reason I don't have that sort of will power, Megan, not where you're concerned.'

'You don't?' she whispered in blank amazement.

'You can ask that?' His incredulous glance moved across her face.

Ask it? She was tempted to ask for it in writing.

'Considering,' he continued heavily, 'that your condition is due to the fact I don't think with my brain around you, I'd have thought you'd have realised that.'

Megan tried to temper the hot thrill she got from his blunt admission by reminding herself that he was talking sex, not love. The wild, raw sex he was discussing was a temporary condition. She was pretty certain he would consider it a temporary insanity.

'Well, anyway, I'm not filthy rich…not in the way you mean.'

His brows arched sardonically. 'There's more than one way?'

She flashed him an unamused grin. 'Dad left Mum well provided for, but the bulk of his estate went to me,' she admitted. 'But I don't take any money out of the estate,' she went on to assure him. 'I went over things with John, and he explained that Dad ploughed the money back into the estate. He managed to do a lot over the years but when he bought the place it was really run down; there's still a lot of work to be done.'

'I thought your family had lived in the place since for ever?'

'They have, but Dad's grandfather had to sell the place to pay off death duties. Dad bought it back years later when he'd made his money. I suppose he wanted to make sure that history didn't repeat itself—that's why he handed the place over to me years before he died. Up until now it hasn't really been feasible for me to live there on a permanent basis. John will be pleased that I'm moving back,' she reflected thoughtfully.

That name again. 'Just who the hell is John?' he demanded.

A perplexed frown pleated Megan's brow. *'John…?'* The overt hostility Luc was radiating bewildered her. 'John is the estate manager. To be honest I don't know how we'd cope without him,' she confided. 'He's been totally marvellous—a tower of strength.'

More muscle than brain, Luc translated. Why did women go for men like that? 'I'm sure he is,' he agreed pleasantly. He probably thought marrying the owner would be a good career move.

Megan warmed to her theme. 'The hours he puts in are unbelievable; I sometimes feel quite guilty,' she admitted.

'So your mother's been running the estate for you…with the help of John?'

'Gracious, no, she'd *hate* that. When Dad died, John just carried on running things. He's very committed. He runs things by me but I trust him implicitly.' The hints he'd been making recently about retiring were a source of concern. There were not many like John out there—plenty of people with impressive paper credentials but not many with a genuine love of the land.

'And how did your mother feel about all this?'

'How do you mean?'

'Being effectively disinherited. Being out of the loop?'

'Relieved,' Megan said immediately.

Luc looked sceptical and, annoyed by his response, she pushed home her message.

'You can take the girl out of the city…' Her slender shoulders lifted expressively before she went on to explain. 'Mum got married and moved into the place with Dad when she was eighteen. She *tried* to love it because he did. Dad,' she recalled with a reminiscent smile, 'almost threw a fit when she suggested moving into a vacant cottage on the estate.'

'That must have put a lot of pressure on their marriage,' Luc observed.

'Not really, they were both prepared to compromise. Dad bought the house in town and spent time there even though he hated it. He said if Mum could spend time in a drafty old pile with bad plumbing, he could put up with London traffic and fashionable dinner parties.'

She knew she'd lost him before she'd reached the end of her explanation. Luc had tuned her out.

She watched as he ran his fingers along his jaw. His expression indicated his thoughts were not just elsewhere…but another solar system.

'This changes things.'

'It *does*…?' she said, expectant. *What?*

He flicked her an impatient look. '*Obviously*. If we're not going to get our own place together, I suppose the logical alternative would be for me to move in with you.'

Mouth open, she looked at him in disbelief. Had he really said *logical*…?

'Did I miss something…? Get a place together? Since

when were we getting a place together?' Had he planned on mentioning this at some point? she wondered…

'Ah.' His speculative gaze skimmed her face. 'You were thinking of marriage?'

She gasped. 'No, I was *not* thinking of marriage!' she denied, turning prettily pink.

'Most women are,' he observed, 'no matter what they say to the contrary. Are you telling me it hasn't even crossed your mind?'

She directed a narrow-eyed look at the tall, lean figure sprawled on the sofa; his contemptuous attitude made her want to hit him. 'No, it damn well hasn't! I can't think of anything more stupid than marrying someone you have not the slightest thing in common with.'

'Outside the bedroom…' Megan froze at this soft addition, her eyes sealed with his brilliant cynical gaze…and beyond the cynicism was a primitive hunger that made the core of heat in her stomach tighten.

His sensual mouth twisted. 'Not that we made it to the bedroom.'

By sheer force of will she made herself smile back as though the subject were one that amused her. Inside her head she could feel every inch of his hard, vital body pressed up against her. She had perfect recall of every insane, intoxicating moment up to and including the moment of shattering climax. If he asked, she'd do it again in a heartbeat. This insight really shook her.

'I didn't come here to ask you to make an honest woman of me,' she croaked contemptuously.

'Why did you come here, Megan?'

'Do you need to ask?' she exclaimed indignantly. 'Fine! I came because I thought you had a right to know about the baby, and I'm not cold enough to send news like this via an email. The fact is I wouldn't marry you if you came gift-wrapped!'

'That makes you my sort of woman. *The fact is,* Megan, I've been married once and I'm not very good at it.'

She widened her eyes and, not wanting to drop Uncle Malcolm in it, feigned ignorance. 'You were married…?' *My sort of woman…* If only that were true, she thought sadly. How different this would feel if she were carrying the baby of the man who loved her.

He nodded. 'For ten years.'

This time her surprise was genuine. Ten years was a long time! 'You must have been very young,' she observed.

'I was twenty, Grace, my wife, was a couple of years older.'

'Were you unfaithful?

There was a startled silence during which Megan wished herself anywhere but here and now. *Me and my wretched tongue!*

'No, I was never unfaithful,' he said, scanning her flushed face, his glance lingering longest on the full soft contours of her mouth. He pressed back harder into the seat; it was getting increasingly difficult to ignore the voice that urged him to part those delicious rosy lips and slide his tongue inside her mouth.

'But I was a lousy husband,' he framed matter-of-factly, 'who wasn't there when my wife needed me.'

A comment like that and you'd have to be not human not to be curious, but from the closed expression on Luc's face and his body language as he picked up his mug of tea it was obvious that, as far as he was concerned, the subject was closed.

I'll respect his privacy, she decided.

Almost as soon as she had made this resolve, a sudden thought came to her that made it impossible for her to honour it. 'Did you and your wife…did you…have you got any children?'

Why hadn't she thought of this earlier? She had been assuming parenthood was as new an experience for him as it was for her, when for all she knew Luc might have a brood of children already!

'Grace was pregnant once,' he told her without any discernible expression in his voice, 'but she lost the baby.'

He'd come to realise that by that point in their marriage they had drifted so far apart that the prospect of the baby had been the only thing holding them together. Perhaps if he'd spent more time with Grace and less trying to make money to buy her the pretty things she loved things might have turned out differently. The irony was he had hated the job that he had put before his wife.

Megan felt the deep, abiding pain behind his pragmatic words as if it were her own. She wanted to hold him so badly it hurt.

'I'm so sorry.' The trite response was wildly inadequate, but she couldn't think of anything else to say.

His bleak eyes narrowed on her face. 'She had a fall,' he supplied without her asking.

It had been at the height of the scandal and the press pack, who had been after blood—specifically his—had latched onto the personal tragedy. Without anyone printing anything libelous, they had managed to intimate that there was a question mark over the accident.

Had the wife fallen or had she been pushed? Grim statistics about domestic violence would coincidentally appear on the same page. The fact he had been in Spain trying to locate his treacherous partner at the time had been no obstacle to a good rumour.

'That must have been terrible for you both.'

'Maybe it wasn't meant to be,' he reflected. 'The baby had a congenital abnormality; they picked it up on a scan. Nothing life-threatening or anything—a cleft palate.'

Megan nodded. She had a friend who had been born with the condition, not that you could tell—the surgery she had had as a child had been very successful.

'Grace,' he recalled in a voice wiped clean of all emotion,

'wanted to have the pregnancy terminated when they told us. She couldn't stand the idea of having a baby that wasn't perfect,' he explained.

Megan tried not to let her natural repugnance to the idea show on her face. You couldn't judge another person's actions without standing in their shoes, her father had always said, and he was right. Who knew what pressures the other woman had been under?

'But she changed her mind.'

'I changed it for her,' Luc admitted. 'And in the end she lost him anyway. If I hadn't pressured her she wouldn't have had to go through the pain and trauma of a miscarriage.'

'It wasn't your fault!' Megan protested, horrified by this insight into the burden of guilt he carried with him. 'It was an accident, a terrible accident,' she added, her voice thick with emotion.

Her spontaneous outburst brought his eyes to her face. The tears trembling on the end of her dark lashes made his jaw clench. 'Please don't go all soft and understanding on me, Megan.'

His sardonic sneer, the sudden cold hostility in his manner, made Megan tense.

'I can see you're just aching to be a shoulder for me to cry on. Frankly I don't have any use for your pity. And before you suggest therapy, I'm totally in touch with my feelings,' he pronounced caustically. 'And I don't believe in living in the past or pointlessly dwelling on things I have no ability to change.'

To have her sympathy thrown back in her face was incredibly hurtful. Megan instinctively hit back. 'If you're so *over it*...' she gave a derisive snort and sketched invisible inverted commas in the air '...tell me how is it you got writer's block when your wife wanted a divorce?'

His eyes narrowed to suspicious slits. 'How would you know that?'

Oh, God! She felt as if guilt were written all over her face. 'Never mind how—'

'Oh, but I do mind,' he cut in silkily. 'I'm assuming you've had a heart-to-heart with Malcolm…' An icy note of menace entered his voice as he added softly, 'Just exactly what did Malcolm tell you?' His expression was so savage that Megan began to feel concerned for her uncle.

'Malcolm didn't tell me anything…well, he might have mentioned in passing that you had got divorced.'

'So you already knew I'd been married?'

She nodded. 'And don't blame Uncle Malcolm; he didn't want to tell me where you were. In fact he refused point-blank until I told him about the baby. He was pretty shocked.'

'And exactly who else knew about the baby before me…?'

CHAPTER THIRTEEN

MEGAN stuck her chin out. She was getting pretty cheesed off with Luc's attitude. 'I told my mother,' she announced. 'Do you have a problem with that? Actually, I don't care if you do because what I do or don't do is none of your damned business. You may prefer to grit your teeth and be a *man* when your life falls apart, and I'd be the first to defend your right to behave like a total prat.' She paused briefly for breath; she was so mad that she was shaking.

At any other time the gobsmacked expression on Luc's face might have made her laugh, but right now she was too angry to see any humour in this situation.

'But when I'm upset,' she continued, '*I* talk to people, the people who care about me!' She swallowed as her voice developed a wobble. 'They'd be hurt if I didn't.'

For a moment Luc sat there watching her struggling not to cry. 'That's some temper you have.'

She sniffed and found a tissue placed in her hand.

'Thank you. I'm generally considered to be a pretty placid sort of person.'

He grinned. 'Sure you are.'

'It's not me,' she protested. 'It's you! You just...' The tissue between her clenched fingers mangled as she struggled to come up with a suitable definition for what he did to her. 'You're hopeless,' she pronounced irritably.

'And you're delicious.'

Her mouth fell open at the unexpected tribute. *Delicious...?* For God's sake, don't start reading too much into it, she cautioned herself.

'I'm glad you had people to share this with over the past few weeks, Megan,' he continued as though he'd not said anything out of the ordinary. 'You're lucky you have people who care about you.'

'People care about you…or they would do if you let them!' She was going to have to stop blurting out the first thing that popped into her head. 'That is…'

Without warning he leaned across and brushed a strand of soft honey hair from her brow. This time he made contact, his touch was brief, but enough to send a shiver of intense longing through her body…

'Don't worry too much—there are still one or two people who are prepared to put up with me.' It had been a brutal method of learning who your real friends were, but he did have a group of loyal friends who had stood by him during the scandal.

Megan flushed. She felt a total idiot—of course he had friends!

'And would you be one of those people who cared if I let you, Megan?'

Megan stiffened and felt her heightened colour intensify until she felt as though she were burning up. She was going to have to learn to guard her tongue in the future.

'Well, you're my baby's father; it would be better if we learnt how to get on.'

'That's a reply but not to the question I asked.'

'It's the only reply you're getting.'

Her grim retort drew a reluctant bark of laughter from Luc. Then his expression hardened. 'Grace and I separated not long after she lost the baby, but we wouldn't have if the baby had survived.'

'Can you be so sure?' Megan wanted to know.

Luc responded without hesitation with a firm nod of his dark head. It would have taken compromises but he would have made it work. 'A child needs two parents, whether they are married or not is irrelevant,' Luc announced, nursing the hot drink between his big hands. 'What matters is that they operate as a single unit where that child is concerned.'

'I think they call that a family. Hardly a new concept, Luc.'

While she respected his views, and even shared them, there was no way she would countenance going along with what he planned. Her smooth brow creased, she searched his lean face. It was weird—while she felt emotionally and physically drained by this difficult scene, now that it had sunk in that he was going to be a father Luc appeared incredibly energised. Never an easy man to say no to, he looked so charged up and resolute at the moment that she knew it was going to be difficult to make him recognise that his idea was a non-starter.

'Like they say, if it ain't broke don't fix it,' he quoted. 'Families work.'

'Not all families are nice or safe places to grow up in,' Megan pointed out gently.

His eyes narrowed on her face. 'But yours was?'

She nodded. 'I was very lucky,' she agreed.

'Would you deny your child what you enjoyed?'

She gave a sigh of frustration, he was trying to tie her in knots and mostly succeeding. 'It isn't the same thing,' she gritted.

'Why?'

Her eyes slid evasively from his. 'My parents loved one another.'

'I loved my wife...' Or thought he had. Lately he had begun to appreciate that what he and Grace had shared had been an infatuation, strong, but not long-lasting.

His honesty had inflicted more pain than she would have believed mere words could.

'But *love* isn't a magic formula for happy ever after,' he continued. 'My father brought me up alone. He didn't have any option—my mother died when I was ten.' His dark lashes swept downwards, making it impossible for her to read his expression. 'I don't want that for my child.'

This explained his determination to make sacrifices for

his unborn child. The image of Luc as a small boy without a mother flashed across her vision and immediately Megan felt the sting of tears behind her eyelids. Maybe it was her newly awakened maternal instincts that made her empathise so strongly with the motherless child? Then again, she had grown to accept that all her emotional responses seemed to be heightened where Luc was concerned.

'Are you all right?' His deep voice held a rough note of concern.

She blinked to clear her blurred vision. Her throat ached as she shook her head and tried to get a grip. 'God, yes, I'm fine. Totally fine,' she assured him, smiling to illustrate the point.

'When did you last have anything to eat?' He gave a self-condemnatory grimace. 'I should have thought.'

Megan pushed her hair behind her ears. 'I had something on the motorway.' The *something* had been a sandwich, which had tasted like plastic; she had left most of it untouched on her plate.

'That was hours ago.'

'Was it?' The last twenty-four hours had been such a blur that she had lost all sense of time.

His searching scrutiny took in the dark shadows beneath her big china-blue eyes. 'You're running on pure adrenaline, aren't you?' he accused.

'Please don't fuss—I hate being fussed.'

Her frown deepened ominously as he talked right across her petulant complaint. 'You've got to look after yourself now,' he reproved.

'I do…I am…'

'How about an omelette? You sit there…better still, lie there, and I'll…'

As he began to rise Megan reached out and caught him by the wrist. She lifted her eyes to his and thought she saw something move at the back of Luc's eyes as he stared fixedly at the pale, slim fingers curved over his much darker skin.

Self-consciously she let her hand fall away and struggled to regain her composure.

The muscles in Luc's brown throat rippled as he swallowed hard, but still he didn't meet her eyes.

'I couldn't eat now…not with things the way they are.'

He turned his head and their eyes locked, smoky grey on shimmering blue. Megan's breathing slowed, everything slowed as she registered the build-up of tension in the air around them.

Even in the privacy of her own thoughts Megan was reluctant to use the only adjective that could begin to describe this dangerous tension—*sexual*. It had a tactile quality and like an invisible envelope it enclosed them in a highly charged bubble.

'The way they are…?'

The throaty rasp of his voice vibrated through her. 'I'm sorry that you didn't have the sort of upbringing every single child deserves, but proposing that we set up home together is no solution. You can't realistically expect us to pretend that we are a couple…?' She shook her head. 'It's a crazy idea. I can't even believe you're suggesting it.'

'I don't want my child growing up with a father he sees every other weekend. I want to be an integral part of his life.'

'I appreciate that,' she said softly. 'But you have to see that living under the same roof, but leading separate lives, is a non-starter even in a house as big as Underwood.'

He frowned. 'Who said anything about leading separate lives?'

Megan went pale. 'Well, naturally I just assumed…' She swallowed and directed a questioning look at his chiselled features. 'You're not serious…?'

'I'm deadly serious,' he assured her grimly. 'Actually I've never been more serious in my life.'

Megan lifted a hand to her spinning head. 'You want us to *live* together…? Live together like…share the same…?' She gulped and began to shake her head vigorously.

'Isn't that what I've been saying? It's the practical solution.'

'I don't want to be practical,' she wailed. 'I want…' Her eyes lifted to his and she stopped dead just before she blurted out the forbidden, *I want you to love me!*

Luc wasn't sympathetic. 'You don't want to be pregnant but you are; people do things they don't want to all the time.'

Megan found this contention deeply depressing, she had to assume that living with her came under the heading of *Things he didn't want to do*. His what's-your-problem attitude stemmed from the fact he was willing to do anything for the sake of his unborn child.

There were any number of flaws in his reasoning, which Megan suspected had more to do with emotion than common sense, but she had to admit he made his case pretty effectively. If she said no she would be putting her own selfish needs before those of their unborn child. She took a couple of deep breaths to calm herself.

'What about love?'

Luc studied her in silence for a moment before responding, 'You want me to say I love you?'

'I want you to consider the very real possibility that one or both of us will fall in love for real at some point. What's that going to do to our child?'

'I'm not going to fall in love with anyone.'

'It's not something you plan.' She could attest to this personally. Had she planned to walk into that flat and find a man who would change her life totally? 'And you may have given up hope of finding a soulmate, but I haven't.'

Luc's regard became cold as stone as his eyes narrowed on her flushed defiant face. 'Did you have anyone in particular in mind?'

Megan frowned; his soft query confused her. 'I don't know what you mean.'

'He wouldn't happen to be called John, would he?'

'John? I don't know any—' She broke off, a bubble of laughter forming in her throat. 'John…you mean John Saxon, my estate manager?'

How many *Johns* did she want? he wondered sourly. 'The John who runs the estate single-handed, the one who is waiting your return with bated breath.'

'John is very attractive, but he celebrated his sixtieth birthday last year. It was a great night—his wife, three sons and eight grandchildren were all there,' she said, taking malicious pleasure from the bands of dark colour that appeared across the angles of his cheekbones.

'Were you jealous? My God!' She gaped, studying his face. 'You were, weren't you?'

Luc's mouth thinned. 'I don't want another man bringing up my child.'

'Well, there's not much chance of that happening in the near future,' she admitted.

'So you're not planning on falling in love?'

'That's an extremely stupid question.'

'Humour me and answer it.'

'Like I already told you, it's not the sort of thing you plan,' she retorted, studying her feet. 'But as I can't rule it out totally at some future date,' she lied, 'you'd better get used to the idea.'

His eyes narrowed to slits. 'I don't damn well want to get used to the idea!'

'That's not a very sensible attitude.'

'*Sensible!*' His sensual upper lip curled in derision. 'Sense doesn't come into any of this. No buts,' he added before she had even opened her mouth. 'Just sit there and be quiet while I make you some food.' He scanned her face with an unnerving laser-like intensity before pronouncing, 'You look absolutely awful.'

Luc was efficient in the kitchen, but then, she thought, he did everything efficiently. The omelette, which he filled with mushrooms and chives from a pot on the window ledge, was delicious. The crusty bread he spread with butter was equally tasty.

Luc brought the food to her on a tray, which she balanced on her lap. He didn't eat; he just sat and watched her, which ought to have put her off, but once she started eating Megan discovered she was so ravenous that nothing could stop her enjoying her impromptu meal.

'Thank you, that was delicious,' she said primly when her plate was clean.

'I feed all the women I get pregnant.'

The self-recrimination in his voice made her frown. 'I don't blame you you know.'

He removed the tray and shot her a strange look. 'I know you don't.'

Megan puzzled over his somewhat enigmatic response as she listened to him banging things in the kitchen area. After a long, exhausting drive and all the days tension, a full stomach and the warm fire had a predictable effect.

She'd just close her eyes for a few moments.

The next thing she knew the room was in darkness. Her fingers touched an unfamiliar throw that was laid over her. Totally disorientated, Megan sat bolt upright with a start.

'Don't panic,' a voice in the darkness soothed.

It all came flooding back. 'I fell asleep.'

'That you did.' Luc flicked the switch of a table lamp and a gentle glow illuminated the big room.

'Why didn't you wake me up?'

She ran a hand over her hair and found one side was sticking up. She tried to pat it down. Luc was the sort of person who didn't get sticky-up hair; he was the sort of person who managed to look perfect no matter the situation.

Now was no exception to this rule. Looking at him, she was engulfed by a wave of longing so intense it hurt.

He looked amused by the question. 'For what reason?'

'Well, I can't drive back home tonight…' Her glance drifted towards a darkened window. 'What time is it anyway?' she wanted to know.

'Ten.'

'What?' she groaned, pushing aside the throw. 'I'll never find a hotel room now.'

'There's a perfectly good bed upstairs.' He saw her expression and he gave a cynical smile. 'And a perfectly good sofa here, which I will take, and,' he added, 'there are clean sheets on the bed.'

Megan was not happy with the arrangement but she accepted the inevitable with as much good grace as possible under the circumstances.

There were no blinds on the roof windows in Luc's big bedroom so she could lie in bed and see the stars above. She could also see the time on the dial of her watch.

She consulted it now and found that it was three-thirty, five minutes later than the last time she had looked! Perhaps a drink of milk might help…?

The getting of the milk involved going downstairs where Luc was sleeping. But, she reminded herself, Luc sleeping wasn't a problem—it was Luc awake that she had to worry about.

Without switching on the lights she slipped quietly downstairs. She winced and froze warily when the electric light from the fridge spilled out into the dark room. Tensely she waited…but no voice in the dark demanded to know who was there…

Clearly Luc was a deep sleeper.

Obviously she was relieved. She didn't *want* him to wake up and find her there; that would be *really* stupid.

Her foot on the bottom step, she stopped and turned back… *Impulse…?* Isn't this what you planned to do all along? Her heart was beating so fast she was sure it would wake the sleeping man. *Isn't that what you want…?*

With a frown she dismissed the intrusive voice in her head and stood looking down at the shadowy sleeping figure. She couldn't see his face, but the blanket spread over him had fallen down to waist level as he slept, revealing that he was naked at least from the waist up. Below…? *Do not go there, Megan!*

She looked with longing that made her throat ache at the smooth, supple line of his strong back and the deliciously defined musculature of his broad shoulders. The muscles low in her belly cramped.

What am I doing? She pressed a hand across her tight, aching breasts. *If he woke up now what would she say? I couldn't resist a quick peek…?* In the darkness a flush of mortification spread over her skin.

She was literally about to turn away when a deep voice enquired, 'Well, are you going to stand there all night, or are you going to get in?'

Megan froze like a startled animal caught in the beam of a strong headlight as Luc flipped over onto his back.

'You're awake,' she gasped stupidly.

'Of course I'm awake.' The scathing derision in his voice was mingling with a distinguishable note of strain.

In the semi-darkness their eyes locked.

Still holding her gaze, he flung back the thin blanket and Megan saw that his naked state extended below the waist. Her entire body started to shake; even in this light there was no mistaking his state of arousal.

'There's no room,' she protested weakly.

'Underneath me…on top of me…'

Megan gave a low moan of sheer lustful longing. She pulled the tee shirt he had given her over her head in one smooth motion. She stood poised, her pale body gleaming translucently and heard his sharp intake of breath.

'Your feet are cold and you're shaking!' he said as she slid in beside him.

'So are you,' she discovered. 'You have no idea how much I have wanted to touch you,' she admitted, running her hands over the lean, smooth contours of his body and making him shake a lot more.

'Tell me about it,' he invited.

Megan did.

At some point in the night he carried her upstairs to the big bed.

When she complained that the bed had gone cold Luc laughed throatily and said that there was a tried and tested method of warming up a bed.

As he pulled her beneath him and touched her in her most secret places with a skill that was simply devastating she wondered if he had utilised his bed-warming skills with anyone else in this particular bed.

She pushed aside the intrusive question and let the tension flow from her body. Why spoil what was perfect by wanting more? What Luc was giving her was more than she had ever imagined experiencing.

CHAPTER FOURTEEN

Luc, behind the wheel of Megan's car, stopped in the village to fill the car with petrol. Megan took the opportunity to nip to the village shop, which was next door. The place, which smelt of newly baked bread, was amazingly well stocked. Megan peered at the amazing selection of cheese and cooked meats in the cold cabinet and the attractively displayed local organic vegetables, commenting on the fact to the woman behind the counter.

'If we want to encourage people to shop locally and not go to the big supermarkets in town we have to give them what they want.'

This sounded like good business sense to Megan, who left with some locally produced cheese, which the woman had personally recommended, as well as the two fat Sunday newspapers she had come in for.

Luc was sitting in the car waiting for her when she got back, drumming his fingers on the steering wheel. She slid in beside him. They had agreed to drive in shifts—at least, she had agreed and he had said nothing at all, which to save argument she had decided to believe equalled assent.

'Where have you been?'

'Like there's so much choice? Though you can get pretty much what you want in the shop. I bought some blue smelly cheese.' Luc laughed when she attempted to read the Welsh label on it.

'I know the one and it is delicious, but you can't have any.'

Megan's chin went up. 'Because you say so.' If he thought he could go around issuing autocratic decrees left

138

and right and she would meekly sit there and take it, he was in for a disappointment.

'Because you're pregnant and pregnant women should not eat, amongst other things, soft cheeses.'

'*Really...?*'

His sensual lips curved upwards. 'Really.'

Megan shook her head; this being pregnant was a minefield. 'How on earth did you know?'

He inserted the ignition key. 'I'm well read, talking of which...' His pained glance touched the pile of newspapers on her knee. 'What do you intend to do with those?'

'Don't worry, I'm not going to eat them. What do you think I'm going to do with them? I'm going to read them.'

'While I'm driving?'

'Well, not while I'm driving.' What was his problem?

'Broadsheet newspapers?'

'You prefer tabloids?'

His lips moved in a spasm of fastidious distaste as she selected a paper and cheerfully tossed the other one over her shoulder. The pages scattered over the back seat. His thoughts were diverted from the unreadable quality of crumpled papers when Megan then crossed her legs, long, sexy, go-on-for-ever legs. She proceeded to balance one edge of the paper precariously on one knee, leaving the other to flap against the driving mirror.

'I'd *prefer* you didn't distract me while I'm driving.' Luc, whose eyes were riveted to the expanse of smooth, rounded thigh her knee-crossing action had exposed, fully appreciated the irony of his comment.

Tight-lipped, she folded the paper with a lot of loud sighs. 'Am I allowed to *talk*?' she enquired spikily when she had disposed of the newspaper in the back seat. She had seen him look at her legs and was excited and trying desperately not to show it.

'I'm a captive audience.'

Megan looked at his hands on the wheel, and a freeze-

frame image flashed across her retina—an image straight
from a fantasy, only it hadn't been, had it…? She really had
sat astride him and pinioned his hands above his head? Not
that he had seemed to mind very much.

The memory of her depravity and how much she had
enjoyed it sent her body temperature soaring by what felt
like several hundred degrees in the space of a single heartbeat.

'I don't feel like talking,' Megan grunted, turning her face
away from him. She looked out the window and tried really
hard to concentrate on the scenery. In direct contradiction
of her earlier comment she almost immediately added,
'About last night…' Did she imagine that his hands tightened on the wheel?

Up to that point neither of them had commented on the
sleepless night they had shared. Megan, exhausted, had
drifted off to sleep near dawn. When she had woken up she
had been alone, a holdall sitting in the middle of the bedroom. Then Luc had walked into the room minus clothes
and modesty!

Megan, who had been taking a sly peek into the bag,
almost fell over. Her eyes had moved in helpless approval
of the sleek, muscular lines of his incredible body. His skin,
still dusted with water droplets had gleamed the colour of
old gold.

A disturbing half-smile had played about his fascinating
lips as he'd continued to towel his dark hair dry.

'I can think of better uses for that towel,' she croaked,
tearing her hungry eyes from his body.

'It's not like you've not seen it all before, and I think
you're wearing enough for both of us,' he commented, turning his amused attention to the blanket she had arranged
sarong-wise to cover herself. 'Nice outfit, but not really suitable for the journey. You'd better get a move on,' he added
casually, flicking the towel in her direction. 'There's a se-
vere gale warning out for later. I don't fancy getting caught

in the middle of a storm. You do remember agreeing to me moving in on a trial basis?'

Last night, she would have agreed to anything he'd suggested. The way she remembered it she pretty much had. Once Luc had got over his concern about sex not harming the baby, he had been pretty inventive.

'I remember everything.'

She still did, which made bringing up the subject now hard, but she had to know.

Luc slowed at a crossroads and squinted up at the signpost partially hidden by a hedge. 'What part of last night specifically did you have in mind?'

'It was all pretty incredible,' she responded with a husky catch in her voice. Beside her she was aware of Luc inhaling sharply. 'At least I thought so…' She took a deep breath. 'I have to know…'

He slid a teasing look at her flushed face and turned left onto a quiet country road. 'If it was good for me?'

She shook her head, then, aware that his attention was on the winding road, explained. 'I have to know if you slept with me because you wanted to get me to agree to you moving in.'

There was a long silence. Megan risked a peek at his profile, it was totally unreadable as he concentrated on the road ahead.

'In a kind of look-what-you'd-be-missing sort of way?'

Megan's heart sank. There was no anger in his voice, his manner was almost indolent, but the deliberate pauses in between his words just screamed with it.

'If that had been my motivation, would it have worked?'

Megan heaved a massive sigh. 'Oh, God, yes…*totally*,' she admitted. 'I have absolutely no will power where you're concerned,' she revealed rashly.

A long sibilant hiss escaped through his clenched teeth, as if this piece of devastating honesty was the last thing Luc had been expecting to hear.

'I had no ulterior motive last night beyond the fact I haven't thought of anything else but having you in my bed since that first time. Does that make you feel better?'

Megan didn't reply, she couldn't, her vocal cords simply didn't function—for that matter nothing else did either. *Better*, he had said! Catatonic might be more apt.

'You've gone awfully quiet.'

'I'm thinking,' she croaked.

'Thinking what?'

'Thinking great sex isn't a sound basis for a long-lasting relationship, but we might as well enjoy it while it lasts.' Megan was pleased that she'd managed to inject the right light-hearted note into her response.

Luc's jaw tightened as he gazed grimly ahead. 'It's going to last a hell of a long time.'

He was wrong, of course; it didn't. Though for a while there she had started believing him, they were the best three months of her life. They were also some of the busiest.

The first month she was still commuting up to London and then the next two months there were the inevitable teething problems that came about from the upheaval of the transfer. She had to work late frequently and arrived home depressed and tired.

Luc didn't complain about the hour or demand to know where she had been. He would take one look at her pale, exhausted face and tell her she looked like hell, then he'd kiss her until the colour returned to her cheeks.

Luc knew a lot about kissing; even thinking about his mouth made her insides melt.

On a typical evening, while she soaked in a scented bath with her non-alcoholic drink he would sit on the edge and sip his wine while he coaxed the details of her days from her. He had a unique ability to make her see the funny side of things that had seemed like major disasters. Then he would tell her about his day, things that had happened in the estate or the entire chapter that had been consigned to the bin.

Like their love making, no two evenings together were the same, but they were all magical to Megan who had never experienced this sort of sharing with anyone before.

The magic was short-lived. At the beginning of November she was searching for a piece of paper that she had scribbled down a friend's change of address on when she saw THE LETTER. She always thought of THE LETTER in capital letters. She had only needed to read one line and the signature: 'I will always love you. Grace.' This had been enough to send her little world crashing around her ears.

Had she imagined that Luc was happy because she was? The irony was she had begun to think lately that he really might actually share her feelings…that he really might be in love with her. On one or two occasions she had even imagined that he had been on the brink of saying something; now she knew for sure that this had been wishful thinking.

Humiliated and hurting, she had taken immediate and drastic action. The result was that she now slept alone in the big bed that they had once shared.

CHAPTER FIFTEEN

'DON'T worry, the boss has already been down,' the man who had been given the roofing contract had said when she'd appeared on site.

Megan's chin lifted at the patronising tone. 'I am the boss,' she told him before she asked exhaustive questions about every detail of the project.

As she made her way back up to the house using the short cut through the wood she turned the interchange over in her head, getting madder and madder. Of course she was glad Luc had fitted into estate life so easily. It was just he fitted in *so* well that there were occasions when she felt as though she was surplus to requirements.

It would have been nice to be needed, she reflected with a self-pitying sigh. As she reached the kitchen door John saw her and came across.

'How are you feeling?' He addressed the question to her bump, not her, but Megan didn't mind this. She had got used to being the uninteresting part of a joint package.

'Fine, thank you.' She patted her stomach with a smile. 'But I'm looking forward to meeting this little one.'

'If you're looking for Luc, he's over at the old stables.'

'Is there a problem, John?' Megan had been as excited as everyone else when a Sunday supplement had expressed an interest in doing a piece on the old stable workshops—work on the extension was due to be finished the next month and this opportunity to publicise the place was heaven-sent.

The newspaper people were due this morning and the last thing they needed was any last-minute hitch.

The older man shook his head. 'Not now. There was a power problem,' he admitted. 'That looked like really throwing a spanner in the works, but that man of yours,' he conceded, 'can turn his hand to most things. He's still got a lot to learn, but he's willing, and he doesn't mind admitting when he's wrong.'

Megan stared at him. Were they both talking about the same man…? The Luc she knew had an inability to even realise when he was wrong, let alone admit it!

'I admit,' John admitted, 'that I had my doubts when he first arrived, but I was wrong. No, I'd say you've got a first-rate man there, Megan, lass.'

Megan just restrained herself from denying ownership.

His comments echoed almost exactly the words her mother had used when they'd spoken on the phone the previous evening—'I hate not being able to see you, but I can relax knowing that Luc is there to look after you, Megan. He really is one in a million.'

'He's driving me mad; he won't let me lift a finger!' Megan complained.

'Isn't that a good thing? I really don't see what your problem is, dear,' Laura responded in a bewildered voice. 'From what you say, he's thrown himself into the place and, quite frankly, supplied what it's been lacking since your father died. I think you've fallen on your feet there.'

Everyone loves Luc, she thought…*including me*. But Luc loves Grace, who loves him right back.

'Oh, yes, he's so busy making himself indispensable around here that we barely see one another. That,' she added bitterly, 'is probably the idea.' Megan listened to the loud silence on the other end of the line and covered her mouth to stifle the groan that rose to her lips.

Her waistline might be a distant memory, she might waddle and not walk, but some things didn't change—such as her unerring ability to say the wrong thing at the even *wronger* time.

'Don't talk nonsense, Megan, the man is obviously deeply in love with you.'

If she hadn't felt so miserable she might have laughed.

'Are you and Luc having problems...?' her mother wanted to know.

'No, we are not having problems,' her daughter gritted. How could you have problems when you never saw one another? When Luc wasn't writing he was busy inspiring admiration and devotion with his enthusiasm. Before she had started her maternity leave it had been easier. Now she saw him all the time and it hurt.

'Because if you are you should talk. It's not good bottling things up.'

On this subject at least her mum was right—things surely couldn't go on like this for much longer. She was pretty certain that Luc was feeling the strain too. Why else did he avoid being alone with her? He was thoughtful, kind, concerned for her welfare, but all this tender loving care was inspired, she was sure, from a strong sense of duty, not love.

At her last appointment with her obstetrician Megan had listened to one heavily pregnant woman confiding to another that her husband expected a medal if he whisked a duster around the living room *and*, she'd complained, barely able to restrain her smugness, '...he can't get enough of me. We've had more early nights than you would believe!'

Megan would have welcomed some slackness with the household chores if Luc had suggested a few early nights, but Luc kept late nights; sometimes it was two or three in the morning when she heard him coming up. She heard him because she was listening out for his tread as he walked past her door. Sometimes as she lay there in the dark, her breath coming fast, she thought she heard his footsteps stop outside her door, but they never did.

Pretending never had been Megan's strong suit. It was ironic really—she had secretly hoped that Luc would fall in love with her and he had actually fallen in love with the damned estate. She had to be realistic: things were not going to change and she would be a fool to pretend otherwise.

Well, he could stay, she'd probably have to contend with a workers' revolt if she asked him to leave, but she couldn't keep up the illusion they were a couple. Luc would probably prefer to stop pretending too, she realised. It couldn't be much fun for him either. If he agreed, he could move into the newly renovated farmhouse by the river next month.

It wasn't ideal, but this situation required some compromise…mostly on her part, admittedly. As far as she could see her plan provided the best of both worlds for Luc; he would be on hand for the baby, but he would be a free agent.

Of course there were drawbacks to this arrangement, especially as his freedom would no doubt involve the reappearance of Grace. So long as he didn't flaunt her under her nose she could cope. After all, they were both adults…

'Is anything wrong, lass?'

Megan pushed aside the nagging concern that her coping mechanisms might not be up to dealing with the reality of Luc having sex with another woman five minutes' walk from where she was sleeping and shook her head.

'I'm fine. The stables, you say…?'

'I suppose you know that this is bribery?'

'So long as it's not extortion.'

Megan, who had taken the shortcut, was halfway through the ivy-covered door when she identified the owner of the ironic tone. She came to a halt and glanced at her wristwatch. How typical—she had finally made a decision and worked up the courage to carry it through and Luc had company. If she hadn't already done the entire I'll-definitely-speak-to-him-later thing and known for a fact that when later came she wouldn't, Megan would have gone back to the house.

'You can laugh about it.' The stranger's voice was lifted in wonder. 'Does this mean we're quits?'

'Let me see,' she heard Luc muse. 'A double-paged feature for a reputation ruined…?' There was a pause and he added in a voice that was chill and contemptuous, 'I don't think so, Malone.'

Megan stepped back into the shadows, feeling guilty as hell for eavesdropping, but unable not to. She had never heard Luc sound like that; she hardly recognised his hard voice. She knew she ought to reveal herself, but 'reputation ruined'—*what was that about?*

'It was nothing personal, Lucas,' she heard the other man placate.

'Strange that it felt pretty personal from where I was standing.'

'Yeah, well…it's a tough old world, and we did print an apology.'

'Two lines on an inside page?'

'All right, I still owe you,' came the reluctant admission. 'But just don't let on I've got a conscience or my career will be over.'

The men must have begun to walk away, because she could hear the deep, distinctive sound of Luc's voice, but, frustratingly, not what he was saying. She stood there for a couple of minutes waiting to be sure that they had gone before she emerged.

Her head was in a whirl. One thing was pretty clear—this newspaper article hadn't been the marvellous piece of unsolicited good fortune they had all imagined. Luc had arranged it. Clearly he felt that this journalist owed him for his *ruined reputation* and he was calling in that favour.

Now she owed *Luc* and she couldn't even let on she knew, let alone thank him—not without giving away the fact that she had dragged the story from Uncle Malcolm.

Her mind bent to this new dilemma, she walked through the arch into the courtyard and straight into the solid chest of a tall figure. Even with her eyes closed she would have recognised that very individual scent, a mingling of soap and the warm male and totally unique fragrance of his skin.

Megan's eyes weren't closed. At the moment of collision

she had automatically tilted her face up to him and found herself looking straight into those scarily penetrating eyes of his…eyes that had as many moods as the stormy sea they reminded her of at that moment.

Luc's hands came up to steady her. She was very conscious of them lying heavily on her shoulders.

'Where are you going in such a hurry?'

Megan fought her way out of the soft fog of desire that misted her vision and made her thought processes slow and sluggish. This was physically the closest they had been in several weeks and the desire to lean into his warm, gloriously hard body threatened to overwhelm her.

She was afraid that if she started leaning she might not be able to stop—*ever*! *I miss you,* she wanted to say, which, considering they saw one another every day, was a comment he might find strange.

'Nowhere…that is here…' Oh, God, if I look as guilty as I sound, I'm in *big* trouble.

Luc, apparently satisfied she wasn't going to fall over, allowed his hands to slide down her shoulders.

The feeling of loss as his hands fell away was quite irrational and totally devastating.

'Oh, they've arrived,' she cried, affecting surprise as she observed the signs of activity in the courtyard. 'How are things going?'

'Did you miss that bit?'

Megan gave a panic-stricken gulp and, playing for time, shook her head. 'Pardon…?' Had he known she was there or was her guilt making her imagine things…?

'Did you miss the part of our conversation from your little hiding place?' he enquired politely.

To be caught listening like a naughty child by Luc, of all people, brought a mortified flush to her cheeks.

'Oh, in that case, let me bring you up to date. Malone, the reporter, says it's going well, but he thinks it would go better if our bronzed blacksmith would take his shirt off.'

'Sam!' she exclaimed, momentarily diverted. 'You're kidding.'

Luc shook his head. 'I'm not and neither,' he added drily, 'was Sam when he told them where to go.'

'I can imagine.'

'After ten minutes of negotiation he has agreed to roll up his sleeves. You know, Megan,' he added seamlessly, 'you don't lie very well.'

This wasn't true. She had told him some big fat lies and he had swallowed them hook, line and sinker! But maybe, she thought despondently, that was because he had wanted to believe them.

'Do you suggest I start to take instruction from an expert…?'

'I don't lie to you.'

'No, you just don't tell me anything. And I wasn't hiding,' she added with a defiant sniff.

One satirical brow lifted. *'No…?'*

'No. I came here looking for you.'

'Now that's unusual enough to merit my attention,' he observed sardonically.

She angled a wary look at his lean face. It was hard to gauge his mood, but then it always was. Not only did Luc have mercurial changes of mood, he was very good at hiding what he was feeling. 'I've had an idea that could solve all our problems.'

'It must be quite an *idea.*' he drawled.

So he wasn't trying to pretend they *didn't* have problems. This was good, she told herself firmly. They were being grown up about this.

Megan repressed a very un-grown-up urge to stamp her feet and yell, *It isn't fair!* 'I've just been to see the farm; the roof's almost finished.'

Luc released an exasperated hiss through clenched teeth. 'I *know* it's almost finished; I went down earlier. There was no need for you to go.'

'I wanted to.'

'I don't suppose it occurred to you to take the Land Rover…? Or better still ask someone to drive you.'

'Don't be silly.' The impatient recommendation brought a glint to his deep-set eyes. 'People have better things to do than ferry me around, and it's only a five-minute walk.' To drive that distance seemed to Megan the height of indolence.

'A five-minute walk down a track that has a two-in-one incline and is at the moment slick with several inches of mud.'

'The doctor says exercise is good for me.'

'I hardly think that's what he had in mind.'

'So now you're a doctor too, are you?'

An amused expression settled on his lean, dark features as he took the brunt of her angry glare. 'I've noticed you always get shrill when you're in the wrong.'

'I am not shrill…or,' she added belatedly, 'in the wrong.'

'Yeah,' he agreed, 'I'd noticed that too.' His expression hardened as he went on. 'Since last week's rain that path is lethal. If you slip there's a nasty…what would you say— twenty-foot drop…? Why,' he demanded, drawing a frustrated hand through his collar-length ebony hair, 'do you insist on taking unnecessary risks?

'Risk…what risk?' she scoffed.

His furious glance was drawn to the pale, slender column of her neck. 'It's only a matter of time before you break your damned neck,' he forecast huskily.

Megan, recalling the path, had to admit he did have a point. 'I didn't fall,' she placated. *Nearly* didn't count, did it…? And there was no point winding him up. 'It'll be lovely when it's finished, don't you think?'

'The only lovely thing he could think about at that moment was her neck. A muscle in his lean cheek clenched as his eyes were compulsively drawn to the blue veined delicate hollow at the base of her throat.

'The renovations are a good quality.' His eyes narrowed

suspiciously. 'What's this about, Megan?' he wanted to know.

'So you like the farmhouse?' she persisted, in a doggedly upbeat manner. 'The lovely views,' she enthused. 'And the attic conversion is a very useful space, very versatile. It would make a great studio don't you think?'

'Have you decided to become an estate agent? Is that your grand idea?'

Megan gave an exasperated sigh. Subtlety, she reflected, was wasted on Luc. 'As us living together is not working out I thought it would be a good idea if you moved into the farmhouse when it's finished. That way you'd have your freedom and be near enough to be involved with the baby as much as you liked.'

The fact he hadn't interrupted and had heard her out in attentive silence was, she decided, slanting an enquiring look at his lean, enigmatic face, encouraging. So encouraging she felt like curling up in a foetal ball of misery and crying her eyes out.

Can't live with him can't live without him. The words popped into her head—a cliché maybe, but it was a cliché that was particularly appropriate to her unenviable situation.

'What do you think?' she asked brightly.

His long lashes lowered in a concealing dark mesh over his eyes but he barely skipped a beat before replying, 'I think…no.'

'No what?' Her shoulders lifted and tried to hide her growing desperation. 'Which bit of my idea doesn't work for you?' If he didn't like the farmhouse there were other options—there had to be because she simply couldn't go on this way!

'No as in no, none of it works for me.'

She opened her mouth to protest at his uncompromising response, but Luc got in before her.

'How long were you standing in your little niche eavesdropping?'

The abrupt change of subject threw Megan. When it came to mental gymnastics she had learnt that she couldn't keep up with Luc. It was a waste of time hoping he'd drop it. Once he got his teeth into a subject that was it—he just didn't let go. She shrugged evasively and tried not to look guilty.

'I just happened to be standing there.' This explanation sounded lame even to her. 'You can't just say no like that.' There was more than a hint of desperation in her hoarse addition.

'I just did,' he reminded her.

Megan gritted her teeth. He had to be the *most* infuriating man ever born. 'We have to discuss—'

'So how long did you *just happen* to be standing there?'

His sarcastic enquiry deepened the flush that already stained her smooth cheeks. 'I didn't want to disturb you. It seemed like a private conversation. Now, about the arrangements for your move—'

'No move, no arrangements. The only place I'll be moving is into your bedroom. I'm sick of being stuck out in Siberia in more ways than one.' While she was still digesting this extraordinary statement he seamlessly picked up the previous topic. 'So you decided to listen in—don't feel too bad about it. It's a perfectly normal response. I just want to know how much you heard.'

'So you can fill in the blanks…?' Her lips twisted in a self-derisive grimace.

It was so unfair, she reflected despondently. She obsessively craved details about his life, but, with very few exceptions, the things she had picked up about him she had gained second-hand. Even during the time when they had been close he had held back.

Luc shared nothing of himself with her and she wanted to know everything there was to know! Some of her thirst for knowledge bordered on the masochistic, especially in matters concerning his marriage and his wife. Did he still talk to her? Did he keep all her letters?

But she would have settled for the silly little things like how old had he been when he learnt to ride a bike? What was his favourite flavour ice cream? What did he think about when he went on his long, solitary walks?

She wanted to know so much, but she knew so little, and yet it seemed to her that Luc knew all her secrets...all except one. And if he refused to move out of the house, she suspected it was only a matter of time before he found that out too! Well, one place he wasn't going to move was her bedroom—pretty obvious she had misheard that casual insertion, but she had to check it out...

'Did you just get all Alpha male and announce you were moving back into my bedroom?' Her mildly amused tone invited him to correct her.

Luc, his expression stony didn't respond to her smile. 'You can move into mine if you prefer.'

'Why would you want to share a room with me?'

One darkly delineated brow rose to a satirical angle. 'Why does a man normally want to share a room with a woman?'

Was he trying to be deliberately cruel? 'The normal hardly applies in this instance.'

Luc's face darkened with displeasure as he noted the resigned expression on her face as she scanned her own ripe body.

'Or are you worried about what Uncle Malcolm will think when he comes to stay next week?' The probability that this was all about keeping up appearances brought a despondent slump to her shoulders.

The same potentially awkward situation had arisen at Christmas when her mother and Jean Paul had come to stay. It had been Megan who had come up with a solution. Luc's response when she had assured him she would sleep on the camp-bed in the dressing-room had been scathing.

'Why not go the whole hog and sleep on the floor?' he'd suggested. 'It makes about as much damned sense.'

Megan had talked him round eventually, though he'd insisted on being the one to sleep on the camp-bed, and he hadn't pretended to like it—but then what man of six four was going to like the idea of sleeping on a narrow put-you-up bed. She hadn't liked it either, but it had been better than the alternative. It had been bad enough with her mother dropping broad hints abut weddings without having to field awkward enquiries about their sleeping arrangements.

'Uncle Malcolm really isn't going to notice,' she reassured him. 'Besides, I think he already knows you only moved in because of the baby. And you can't possibly sleep on that camp-bed again.'

Luc's long lashes came down over a gleam of anger. 'I wasn't intending to sleep on the camp-bed.'

'Well, normally I'd take my turn but it would probably collapse under my weight.'

'You're not sleeping on it either.'

'But—'

'And Mal's not coming,' he revealed casually.

'Of course he's coming.'

Luc shook his head. 'No, I explained to him that you're not up to visitors.'

For a moment Megan stared at him in open-mouthed incredulity. *'You what...?'* She expelled a wrathful pent-up breath in one long, sibilant hiss. 'How dare you tell him that!? She pressed her fingers to her temples where she felt the blood throbbing. 'I'm absolutely sick of being treated like a child. You,' she declared, stamping her foot, 'have absolutely no right whatsoever. You're not my husband.'

Luc's glance lifted. A look she couldn't quite pin down flickered briefly across his face. 'If I was, would that mean you'd do what I suggested?'

She released a scornful laugh. *'In your dreams!'*

'I thought as much.'

'And you don't suggest, you issue proclamations and expect everyone else to meekly follow them.' Most people, as far as she could tell, did just that. His orders might have been concealed behind a smile and a laid-back attitude but, as far as Megan was concerned, they were still orders. 'I don't respond well to authority.'

'Why, you little rebel, you.' His thin-lipped taunt drew a gurgle of rage from her clamped lips. His brows lifted in enquiry. His phoney smile faded as he added, 'Look, I'm not going to apologise for looking after your best interests, Megan. You need plenty of rest; remember what the doctor said.'

The occasion a couple of months earlier when she had turned up at his bedroom door in the middle of the night had borne no resemblance to the fantasy he had polished and nurtured over the weeks since they had shared a bed. The fear in her eyes when she had sobbed she was losing the baby would stay with him for ever.

'Among other things, I remember he said it would be advisable for me to refrain from sex,' she reminded him, flushing.

It had seemed pretty ironic at the time. Luc had been suitably supportive, dismissing the burden of celibacy with a shrug of his magnificent shoulders. But he had grilled the unfortunate medic on every possible aspect of her condition and treatment.

She didn't have a condition, the doctor had said, her blood pressure was slightly raised and she was, quite simply, exhausted. The treatment he had recommended was rest and plenty of it. The slight blood loss that had alarmed her, he went on to explain, was most probably not significant. It happened to a lot of women and he was merely erring on the side of caution.

'Most probably' was not a phrase that Luc had been happy with, and he'd had no qualms about sharing this with the doctor. The GP, who usually had an air of reassuring calm, had looked in need of some rest himself by the time he had finally managed to get rid of Luc.

'Do you think I'm going to leap on you Megan? You've made your feelings on that subject perfectly plain and I'm not in the habit of forcing myself on women who find my touch repulsive.'

'Of course I don't think you'd do that,' she retorted flushing.

'Haven't you ever wanted to hold someone?' He broke off and turned away.

'You don't want to hold me; you want to hold...'

Luc swung back and the expression of ferocious anger in his taut face shocked her.

'What are you talking about?' He heard the breathy whisper of her forlorn sigh and his anger slipped away.

CHAPTER SIXTEEN

THERE was an unusual air of indecision about the habitually assured Luc as he ran a hand down his jaw. The frown line between his darkly defined brows deepened as he met her wary eyes.

'Megan, you're beautiful and you are carrying my child! But I have never felt my child move,' he continued in a thickened, impassioned voice. 'I have never held you in my arms at night, and felt my baby kick.' His glance lowered to her belly.

Just as Megan felt she could not take that long, dragging silence for another second without screaming, Luc's long lashes lifted from the curve of his razor-sharp cheekbones. The raw expression glittering in his deep-set eyes made the breath catch painfully in her throat.

'You have erected a wall—a damned ten-feet-high three-feet-thick wall—between us.' He spread his expressive hands to illustrate the dimensions under discussion. 'And I've no idea why. One minute we were happy together, the next you act as though I've got the plague.'

This grim accusation startled Megan, who opened her mouth to deliver a horrified denial. She paused; could she deny it? Was there not a grain of truth in his accusation? For the first time she looked at things from his point of view; the things she saw brought a worried frown to her brow. It had been her desire to retain a little dignity that had prevented her from telling him she knew about the letter and about Grace. Now she wasn't so sure it had been the right call.

'Hell!' he yelled into the silence. 'You're not just content to push me out of your bed, now you want me out of the

158

damned house. What is it, Megan—out of sight, out of mind?'

If only it were that simple, Megan thought, shaking her head despondently. Suddenly she couldn't hold her frustration in another second. 'That's the problem—you never are.'

He gave an impatient frown. 'I'm never what?'

'Out of my mind…I think about you constantly.'

Luc froze and took a deep shuddering breath. His hard, probing stare pinned her to the spot and he seemed to be able to see straight into her head. 'You think about me…?'

Megan who was already regretting like crazy her candour, flushed and replied icily, 'Didn't I just say so?'

'Then why the big sell…lovely farmhouse, views-to-die-for thing?'

'I said you're constantly in my head, not that I want you to be there or that I like it!' She bit down viciously on her quivering lower lip.

Luc watched a single tear slide silently down her cheek and cursed softly under his breath. 'For God's sake, don't cry!' he pleaded in a husky voice. 'I just can't bear to see you cry—it kills me!' he confessed, swallowing hard.

She gave a sniff. 'S…sorry.'

Luc swore again and took her hand. Megan's eyes widened. She could literally feel the tension and urgency in his lean body.

His eyes swept across her face. Something in his look made her heart pound. 'We need to talk, but not here.'

Overwhelmingly conscious of the warm fingers curled around her own, Megan walked at his side without protest as he led her along the path to a group of buildings that housed amongst other things, the estate manager's office.

'This should be private enough.'

'Hardly private—what if John comes in?' Apparently whatever Luc had to say was so urgent he couldn't wait to get back to the house? Suddenly she wasn't so sure she wanted to know.

Luc dismissed her complaint with an off-hand shrug. 'John has gone home early,' he said, closing the door of the manager's office behind them. 'I told him to take the rest of the day off. He's picking his daughter up from the station.'

'He didn't tell me.'

'I expect he thought I'd tell you.'

'He probably didn't realise that you don't talk to me any more.'

Luc was in the act of pulling forward a leather-padded swivel chair; at her bitter comment his dark head whipped up. 'What the hell are you talking about? We talk…at least I do.'

'Don't make me laugh!' Megan, closer to tears than laughter, pleaded. 'You can't bear to be in the same room as me!' She heard her voice rise to a shrill, accusing shriek and winced.

A look of blank astonishment settled on Luc's lean, expressive face.

'Did you think I hadn't realised, Luc? *Please.* I may not be as clever as you, but I'm not *stupid.* You're not exactly subtle,' she told him. 'I walk in a room and you remember you need to be some place else. I know that the baby was all you wanted. But I need to be wanted.'

Luc shook his head and released a hoarse laugh of incredulity. 'That's what you think—that's actually what you think…?' Like his voice, the hand he dragged down his jaw was not quite steady.

'I don't *think*, I *know*,' she retorted fiercely.

Muttering darkly under his breath, Luc wheeled the chair towards her and, ignoring her complaints, pressed her firmly down into the leather seat.

'I don't want to sit down.'

Luc, his hands on the armrests, leaned down towards her. The intimate sensation of his warm breath brushing against her cheek made all the downy hairs on Megan's ultrasensitive skin stand on end. A sigh shivered through her body.

'*Tough.*'

Her eyes widened in indignation. 'I'm pregnant!'

'So I have to be nice to you?' One dark brow arched. 'Even,' he added grimly, 'if you go out of your way to be unpleasant to me. *You're* the one who wanted not to have any special treatment just because you're pregnant,' he reminded her.

'You're a bully!'

Her tremulous contention drew a harsh laugh from Luc, who, with a stern warning to, 'Stay put, and shut up,' settled himself down on the desk opposite. He pressed his hands against his thighs and stretched his long legs in front of him.

Megan did as he asked, not from any desire to be co-operative, but because the sheer shock at being addressed this way had literally robbed her of speech. She was just rediscovering her vocal cords when he said something that struck her dumb all over again.

'Are you surprised I can't be in the same room as you under the circumstances?' he wanted to know.

Megan turned the colour of her white shirt and tried not to let him see how much his words had hurt her. 'I suppose not,' she agreed unhappily.

She knew it wasn't uncommon for men to be turned off when their partners were pregnant, but Luc's revulsion seemed to go further. Was it all pregnant women he didn't like being around or just her?

Luc was a very sensual man. It was not logical to expect a man like him to survive without sex. Her dreams were plagued with jealous nightmares of slim, eager women throwing themselves at him and him not ducking! Did Grace still enjoy his bedroom skills? Had they ever stopped being lovers? The not knowing, and the not knowing whether she *wanted* to know, was killing her.

'It's not my fault.' It was, though—she was the one who had chucked him out of her bed.

A spasm of irritation crossed his dark, devastatingly handsome features. 'It's your fault I can't be in the same room as you, you stupid, infuriating, *gorgeous* woman!' he yelled.

Gorgeous? Am I hearing things, or did he just call me…? Her glance dropped to the bulky mass of her body and she shook her head; she had *definitely* misheard.

'*My fault…?*' she said cautiously while noting the dark bands of colour that stained the high contours of his chiselled cheekbones.

'You set the damned rules: separate bedrooms, no sex, just good friends…this ringing any bells?' He broke off, breathing hard, and lifted his hands to his head, sinking his fingers into the dark strands of thick glossy hair.

'The doctor said it wasn't safe…'

'You had already asked me to leave, Megan.'

The man who prided himself on his self-control, his ability to view situations with objectivity, made a visible effort to control himself, but his hardly fought composure slipped again when he encountered her wide shocked intensely blue gaze.

'Dear God, don't look at me like that,' he pleaded hoarsely. 'I respect how you feel at the moment…it's just damn hard.'

'How would you know how I feel?' Please let him not know.

'You told me.'

Megan shook her head. If she had confided her feelings she thought she might have remembered. It occurred to her that they might be talking at cross purposes.

'Did you or did you not say the idea of sex while you're pregnant makes you feel ill?'

Of course she recalled the words slung in the heat of an argument. '*You believed me…?*' She gasped, unable to disguise her amazement.

'There's absolutely no way I'm going to force myself on you; it's just difficult for me to be around you when I want...' He stopped, his vibrant colour fading dramatically as his narrowed eyes darted over the contours of her face. 'You *lied*...?'

Megan barely registered his hoarse question. An extraordinary idea was forming in her head. Dear God, now wouldn't *that* be ironic? I'm sitting one end of the enormous house lusting after him and he's sitting the other...!

The baby chose that moment to remind her of its presence, launching a kick at her ribs so strong that she scrunched up her eyes and cried out softly. It also reminded her that the idea of anyone being driven mad with frustrated lust for her in her present condition was remote, to put it mildly.

The moment the cry left her lips Luc was on his feet. 'Are you all right?'

She opened her eyes and found Luc sitting on his heels at her feet. His lean, strong face was chalk-white, the skin drawn taut with anxiety across his magnificent cheekbones. Megan rubbed a hand across her big belly and smiled reassuringly.

'This one packs quite a punch.'

He visibly relaxed. 'Is he kicking you now?'

She nodded and his fascinated eyes returned to her stomach. 'He could be a she,' she reminded him.

'I'd settle for either.' He stretched out his hand towards her. 'Can I...?'

Megan's eyes dropped to his hand. The tentative quality of his request brought a lump to her throat. By way of reply she caught hold of his wrist and laid his hand against her belly.

'I can't feel anything,' he said, disappointed.

'You will,' she promised just before, on cue, the baby launched a kick, less vigorous than the previous one, but strong enough to make Luc cry out in wonder.

'Does that happen a lot?'

The awe in his voice made her smile mistily. 'All the time.'

'*Good God…!*'

Megan, who found sitting in one position for long made her back ache, shifted her position. Immediately Luc's hand fell away from her stomach.

Instead of straightening up, Luc sat back on his heels and looked at her.

Their faces were almost on a level and there was a quality in his silent, unblinking regard that made Megan deeply uneasy.

'*What…?*'

He responded to her querulous enquiry with an enigmatic smile. Then, after a suitably nerve-racking silence, he revealed the reason for his odd behaviour. 'You said you lied.' She began to shake her head and he added in a voice that brooked no opposition. 'You lied about being off sex.'

Megan's eyes dropped from his. The perceptive clarity of those opaque depths made her ashamed and defensive at one and the same time. 'I might have stretched the truth,' she admitted gruffly.

'Then your skin didn't crawl at the thought of me touching you?'

Her head lifted. 'Did I *really*…?'

He nodded. 'You did. For God's sake, Megan, *why*…? It's been a total nightmare wanting to touch you, hold you…' He released an unsteady groan. 'Of course I couldn't bear to be in the same room as you; I didn't trust myself!' Pure silver, his molten eyes moved hungrily over her features, which pregnancy had made softer and rounder. 'When I think what you have put me through these months I could strangle you!' He took her chin and tilted her face up to his.

The expression stamped on his lean features took her breath away.

'So,' he said, scanning her face with a heart-stopping

blend of fierce hunger and devastating tenderness. 'You fancy me…'

He sounded so unbelievably smug that she grinned. 'Pity,' she said with a rueful glance down at her body. 'It's too late now to do much about it.'

'*Who says…?*'

'Don't be silly,' she retorted. 'Look at me,' she invited.

'You're beautiful, ripe and luscious.'

This husky fulsome praise sent a tidal wave of warmth through her body. 'That's nice to know,' she admitted, blushing rosily. 'But I'm…well…' *Burning up with lust…?*

Luc looked puzzled. 'You're what?' he prompted, sliding his fingers into her hair. With a sigh Megan let her head fall back as he massaged her scalp.

'It isn't just about sex,' he said.

'It isn't?'

'You think I'm that shallow?' he ground out, looking exasperated at her response.

'Not shallow, but you can't tell me it's not important to you.'

'And it's not to you?

Watching the honey strands fall through his fingers, a handful of her rich, plentiful hair in his hand, he lowered his mouth to hers.

The kiss was so tender, so sweetly passionate that the tears sprang to her eyes as she melted into him.

'Why did you say it, Megan?' he demanded as they drew apart. 'Why did you lie to get me out of your bed?'

It was the question she had hoped he wouldn't ask. Megan shook her head mutely and would have turned away had he not taken hold of her chin firmly between his thumb and forefinger.

'*Why…?*'

'I saw the letter; it was lying there,' she admitted huskily.

Luc looked at her blankly. 'What letter?'

'It was an accident. I was looking for my address book,'

she explained stiltedly. 'And...I didn't read it,' she added with an urgent shake of her head. 'But it was open and I saw...I read...' She swallowed and lowered her gaze, too ashamed to look at him.

'I will always love you.' The words had leapt from the page as had the name scrawled at the bottom of the page—*Grace.*

She had not known until that moment that jealousy could be like that, be like a physical pain, a constant gnawing ache that invaded every cell of your body.

Would Luc have got back with his wife if it hadn't been for the child she was carrying? When he'd made love to her at night had he thought abut his ex-wife, had he seen her face when he'd closed his eyes in the moment of release...?

The thought that she'd been a substitute, that while he'd been with her he'd dreamed of being with someone else, was something she just couldn't bear.

Luc was looking mystified. 'What letter?'

'From your...from Grace,' she whispered.

'I get a lot of letters from Grace.'

This was something she could have lived without knowing. Did she declare her undying love in all of them? Megan wondered.

'Considering you're divorced, isn't that a little unusual.'

'She likes to keep in touch, even though she's remarried,' he admitted.

His guarded manner was confirming all her worst fears. 'She's married to someone else now?'

'For the time being.'

Of course, Grace was getting a divorce and she wanted to get back with Luc...who wouldn't? she thought, sliding a covetous look over his long, lean, supremely gorgeous frame. The idea took hold and she felt physically sick. You could be prepared for the worst but when it finally came it still hurt like hell.

'Does that mean that things are not working out for her?'

She was amazed that she could feel so totally wretched and still appear normal.

She realised that she must be faking it really well because Luc didn't appear to have a clue that she was ready to fall apart. He was probably blind to everything else when he thought about his marvellous Grace.

'I told her at the time that…' His shoulders lifted in one of his expressive shrugs. 'But that's Gracie for you.' The rueful tone of his voice increased the icy grip of the fingers that were squeezing her heart.

'She's impetuous?'

He nodded and said with feeling, 'And then some.'

And Megan wanted to head for the nearest dark corner to lick her wounds. Instead she rubbed salt in them by imagining all the outlets for her impetuosity that *Gracie* might have found in the bedroom; or, being impetuous, she probably didn't limit her surprises to one room. They had probably made love in every room of the house.

'The guy's years older than her; he's got children older than she is.'

'A lot of women are attracted to older men. I suppose they offer stability…?'

'It helps if they've got a lot of money stashed away.'

Was he saying his ex-wife had married for money—?

'Don't look so shocked, *chérie*, not everyone is the hopeless romantic you are. Grace is one of ten children; she had a tough life as a kid and just when she had started to get used to having the flashy cars and the big houses it was snatched away from her. She was honest—she couldn't be the wife of a poor man.'

Megan, who had always considered herself the most pragmatic of people, shook her head in protest. 'I'm not a romantic.' A romantic she might not be, but the idea of walking away from your man at a moment when he most needed a wife's support filled her with disgust.

'You haven't asked me how I lost my money…?'

Well, he had plenty of money now, Megan thought. Which meant his avaricious ex was grasping and greedy.

'It's not my business.'

For a long moment Luc scanned her face, then with the deliberation of someone who had come to a decision he pulled out a chair and, spinning it around, straddled it. 'Five years ago I had a successful business and a partner.'

'Yes, you told me.' She gave a quick uninterested smile. 'You hated it, but you made a lot of money…and then lost it.' This moment, the moment when Luc felt able to confide in her, could have meant something very special if she didn't already know what he was going to say. If she hadn't gone behind his back, to Uncle Malcolm.

'Aren't you curious?'

Feeling guilty as sin, she shook her head. 'Not especially.'

'Amazing! You really are the most incredible woman.'

His admiration made her feel worse than ever. 'I'm not incredible at all; I'm terrible!' she wailed, covering her eyes with a hand as she gave a self-condemnatory groan. 'I already know about your partner running off with all the money and the man who committed suicide and how the press were hateful to you.' Megan couldn't look at him.

A short static silence followed her emotional confession. *'Malcolm…?'*

The question had a resigned ring to it and Megan, who had expected him to go ballistic, opened her fingers and peeked cautiously through them.

'It wasn't his fault.'

'No, that I can believe. I have noticed,' he continued drily, 'that when you make up your mind you can be difficult to divert. In fact you can be difficult full stop.'

'Aren't you angry?'

One corner of his fascinating mouth lifted. 'Do you want me to be?'

'No, of course not, it's just I know how you value your

privacy and I know I should have waited until you wanted to tell me.' She bit her lip. 'I wish I had,' she confided huskily.

'If it makes you feel any better, Malcolm supplied me with some information...reluctantly supplied,' he added with a reminiscent grin.

Megan's smooth brow puckered. 'I don't understand.'

'I wanted to know a few things about the creep you almost married.'

'Brian!' she exclaimed, astonished by this revelation. 'Whatever for?'

Megan watched as his white teeth bared in a smile that did not touch his eyes. 'I was kind of curious about what you saw in him in the first place. Now I know. The man is a total creep, but a *pretty* total creep.'

Pretty...? Megan mentally compared Brian's weak chin and average features with the man she was looking at and she laughed; she couldn't help it.

'What's so funny?' he growled.

Megan didn't respond. 'How do you know what Brian looks like?'

'I happened to swing by a bar and he was there.'

Megan's eyes widened. 'You wanted to see him...why?'

Luc passed a hand across his forehead. 'Why the hell do you think...?' His attitude suggested she ought to have found the explanation obvious—she didn't.

'I've not the faintest idea,' she told him.

'I wanted to kick the slime ball's teeth down his throat...' His nostrils flared as he inhaled deeply. 'He hit you,' he gritted.

'And you intended to do what? Hit him?'

'It did cross my mind,' he admitted, rubbing a hand over the stubble on his jaw.

'But you didn't...?' She felt she had to check.

'I got a case of better judgement,' he admitted with the air of someone who regretted the decision. 'I blame it on my dad—he always told me I couldn't pick on anyone smaller than me. The creep only came to my shoulder.'

Megan's eyes dropped from his. 'I'm glad you didn't hit him,' she admitted.

Luc's expression hardened to granite.

'Aside from the fact I really don't need anyone to fight my battles. No big feminist statement,' she promised, 'just plain fact. When I said he hit me, I might have missed out the part where I hit him back…?'

Luc stared at her for a moment, then started to grin. 'You did?'

Shamefaced, she nodded. 'I'm not actually a violent person; it was a reflex action.'

'Did you cause much damage?' he asked with a hopeful expression.

'None that I could see, but apparently the bridge work that needed repairing cost him a packet. He threatened to sue me.'

Luc threw back his head and laughed. 'God, what a prat! You,' he added with an approving warmth that brought a glow to her cheeks, 'are incredible.'

'I know…I mean,' she added hastily, 'I know he's a prat. Landing the punch was more luck than good judgement,' she admitted.

'So now that we have both invaded each others' privacy, I think you could say we're quits?'

'I suppose so.' She looked at the hand he stretched out towards her and after a moment placed her hand in it. The contact sent a neat electric thrill through her body, which she endured with a fixed smile. As soon as it was possible—without causing offence—she removed her hand.

'Now tell me what you read or didn't read in Gracie's letter that made you chuck me out of bed.'

'I know she loves you and you love her.'

'I don't love her.'

'Well, you would say that, wouldn't you?' she countered sadly.

The phone in Luc's pocket began to ring.

Megan, grateful for the reprieve, watched him pull it from his pocket.

'Don't switch it off. It might be important.'

'More important than my infidelity...?' His anger made her wince. *'Patrick,'* he snarled into the mouthpiece.

Megan tapped her toe on the floor as he began to listen. When he responded it was in rapid French. Megan tuned it out; she was quite proud of her grasp of the language, but there was no way she could follow what Luc was saying.

It was only when she heard her stepfather's name that she began to actually listen. She caught Luc's eye and, mouthing, Let me speak to him, held out her hand. Luc shook his head and turned his back on her.

When Luc finally hung up his expression was preoccupied.

'Why didn't you put me on? I wanted to talk to Jean Paul.'

Without replying he caught her hands in his and drew her towards him. His grave expression made her stomach lurch in fear.

CHAPTER SEVENTEEN

'Now don't panic.'

An instruction, Megan reflected, that was guaranteed to make her do exactly that.

'Is it Mum?' Unconsciously her hands went flat to her own belly.

Luc nodded. The compassion in his eyes made her spirits plummet; people didn't look like that when they were about to give you good news.

'The baby...?'

'Your mother is in hospital. They're performing an emergency Caesarean.'

The blood seeped out of her face leaving her skin marble-pale. 'How is she? This is my fault...I should have told her that she was too old to have a baby, but I encouraged her.'

'Cut that out right now!'

His bracing tone made her blink. Dazed, Megan looked from the hands encircling her wrists to his stern dark face.

'This isn't anyone's *fault* and certainly not yours. Laura had every test going; she was given a clean bill.' Megan reluctantly nodded. 'And even if her age was a factor, which we don't know, this was not your call; it was hers and Jean Paul's. You did what you had to; you supported her decision.'

Megan's eyes remained on his face, then after a few tense moments she nodded.

'So you're not going to go all hair-shirty on me?'

Megan exhaled deeply and shook her head again. 'No, what...what happened? Did Jean Paul say?'

'Something to do with the placenta. Jean Paul was...unclear.' The Frenchman had actually sounded as though he was in shock. 'She began to bleed, apparently.' He didn't mention the pain that the distraught Jean Paul had graphically described.

Luc wished he hadn't said as much as he had when Megan literally swayed.

'Come on, now, you shouldn't upset yourself.'

'Don't upset myself? My mother is bleeding to death!' Her voice rose to a shrill, scornful crescendo.

'She isn't…she'll be fine,' he said, hoping like hell he was telling the truth. 'And Jean Paul will ring the moment she gets out of surgery…or they know something. In the meantime we should be positive.'

'*Know something…?*' With a distrustful frown she homed in on his comment. 'What do you mean, *know something*?' Her eyes narrowed into suspicious, accusing slits on his face. 'You mean if she dies, don't you?' She pulled her hands from his clasp and let out a wail that made the hairs on his nape stand on end. 'They think Mum's going to die and you're not telling me everything. I know you're not.'

'I swear I am.'

'Then why didn't you let me speak to Jean Paul?'

Her breath coming in short, frantic gasps, her eyes darted around the room. She reminded Luc of a cornered wild animal.

'He doesn't know any more than I'm telling you, Megan.'

In the midst of her heart-wrenching anguish Megan experienced a sudden icy calm and sense of purpose. She knew exactly what she had to do. She explained it to Luc.

'I have to go to Paris.'

'Megan, you're thirty-seven weeks pregnant; you can't travel.' Luc's expression was compassionate, but his tone was inflexible.

'I'm not asking your permission; I'm telling you what's going to happen.'

'Calm down, Megan, you're not thinking straight.'

'You don't understand,' she accused, backing away from

him. 'I *have* to. She needs me.' Her shoulder blades made contact with the wall and she leaned back against it, glad of the support.

'How do you intend getting to Paris?'

She looked at him blankly.

'You're not thinking straight, Megan.'

'If I catch the next flight…I could be there by…'

He shook his head slowly from side to side. 'They won't let you fly.'

Megan glared at him, leaking self-control from every pore. Why was he making this difficult? 'I'll *make* them. I'll say I'm only twenty…' how pregnant could you be before they wouldn't let you fly? '…something weeks.'

'And even if they would permit it, I wouldn't let you go.'

She looked at him for a moment with real loathing. At some level she was aware that she was being totally irrational but she couldn't stop. 'God, but I hate you!'

Luc flinched as though she had struck him, but not a muscle in his face moved.

'We can discuss your feelings for me at a later date.'

'I don't want to discuss anything with you. I want to see my mother.'

'Listen, I know you're scared and you want to be with your mother, but she has Jean Paul. He's her husband; it's his job to be with her. Your first concern has to be your own health and that of our baby.'

God, he was right! She knew he was *right*. Megan caught her trembling lower lip between her teeth. The antagonism in her eyes faded as their eyes meshed.

'She's so far away…' She closed her eyes, silent tears sliding down her cheeks.

Luc was at her side in a heartbeat. He stroked her hair; his expression was so tender that the trickle of tears became a flood. 'I know,' he crooned, drawing her close.

With a cry Megan collapsed weakly against him, her body shaking with sobs.

Luc had never felt more helpless in his life.

Long after her tears had abated Megan remained where she was in the protective circle of his arms seeking comfort from his strength, the warmth of his hard body, the familiarity of his scent.

It was the sound of the phone ringing that made her break away. She looked at the phone in his hand, her eyes wide and fearful.

'You all right?'

She nodded and even managed a watery smile. 'Go ahead, answer it,' she said, brushing the hair from her damp face with the back of her hand. 'I'll be fine, promise.'

Luc nodded and lifted the phone. After a moment he covered the receiver. 'She's out of surgery and she's fine,' he told her, grinning from ear to ear.

Megan experienced a rush of relief so intense it made her head spin. Weakly she leaned against the wall. 'Thank God!'

'Are you all right?' Luc asked, half listening to the relieved husband's emotional and extremely loud outpouring in his ear.

Megan dug deep into her reserves to give him the ghost of a smile, oblivious to the fact that, far from reassuring him, it scared the hell out of him. When she closed her eyes tight and began to shake, visibly shake, he shoved the phone back into his pocket and crossed the floor to her side in two strides.

He fell onto his knees beside her chair and framed her face in his hands.

'I th…thought…' Her eyes, so big and so intensely blue that he still got a shock every time he looked into them, flickered open.

Luc smoothed the hair from her eyes and pulled her head onto his shoulder. 'I know what you thought,' he said quietly. 'Don't try and talk, just give yourself a minute; you've had a terrible shock.'

For once Megan didn't resent his fussing. 'I'm sorry I yelled at you.'

'Forget it.'

'And I'm really glad you're here.' Her eyes lifted to his. 'I don't know what I'd have done if you hadn't been here.'

Something flickered at the back of Luc's eyes. 'I'll always be here for you, Megan.'

He'll always be here for the baby, she sadly translated. 'I know you will.'

Her eyes suddenly snapped open. Arms pressed against his chest, she pulled upright. *'The baby...?'* she asked fearfully.

'The baby...?' he repeated blankly. Then his eyes widened. 'Oh, the *baby*. Fine, a little small so they're keeping it in an incubator.'

'It? Is it a boy or girl?' Because of her age her mum had had an amnio, but she hadn't wanted to know the baby's sex. Megan didn't think she could have shown the same restraint if she had been offered the same opportunity.

'Almost definitely.'

'No, seriously.'

'I'm not sure...Jean Paul might have said before I hung up on him.'

The outrageous admission made her stare. 'You hung up on Jean Paul!' she gasped. 'How could you? I have to know if I've got a brother or sister.'

'What's the hurry? It'll be the same sex in the morning.'

'Only a man would say anything that stupid,' she told him. 'I'll ring. Give me your phone....' Without waiting for him to comply she reached inside the breast pocket of his shirt where she could see the outline of his mobile.

'It won't do you any good ringing. Jean Paul's phone will be switched off now...it is a hospital.'

'You're probably right.' Megan, who in the last few seconds had realised that the niggly back pain she had had all morning was actually something more, gave a distracted smile.

Everything she had learnt in antenatal class had gone! Her mind was a total blank.

'I was simply prioritising.'

'What could possibly be more important?'

He stilled. What the hell was important to him? Not long ago he wouldn't have had to think about it. It had been doing what he wanted when he wanted.

'Are you all right?' she asked, concerned by the dazed expression that had settled on his lean features.

His eyes focused on her face. His life if he had never met Megan—no drama, no epic battles of will, no spending frustrated nights reading his way through the library.

Megan who had strained to catch his soft reply, shook her head. 'Sorry, what did you say?'

'*You.*' This time Luc's voice was not soft, it was firm and resonant.

He had experienced one of those rare moments in life when all the pieces slotted into place. It wasn't a gentle voyage of self-discovery, more a kick in the pants.

A kick that Luc thought he deserved for taking this long to see something that would have been so obvious! He loved Megan, and loving her wasn't going to change because they got old or were separated. Megan wasn't Grace and he wasn't the kid he had been when he had got married. He needed this woman, without her his life was empty.

He exhaled, then said it again and said with more confidence, 'You, you're the most important thing in my life.'

He means the baby, she told herself, so don't say anything stupid. Their eyes met and she said it anyway.

'If this is your way of saying you have feelings for me, you have very bad timing...' she told him huskily. 'In fact,' she added grimly, 'it's probably the worst timing possible.'

'It feels like a good time to me,' Luc rasped. Unable to resist the temptation of her white smooth neck, he pressed his lips to the pulse spot at the base of her throat. Megan felt his tongue and mouth move up her throat and sank her fingers into his dark hair.

'Luc…?'

'Uh-huh,' he said, not stopping the lovely things he was doing.

'I think we should stop.'

His head lifted. 'If you're worried about making love, don't be. There's more to making love and giving pleasure than penetrative sex. There's touching and tasting and…'

She shook her head. At any other time his frank explanation would have given her a case of terminal embarrassment, or more likely pleasure, but she was beyond that now.

She leaned backwards. 'No, Luc, I'm serious. We have to go.'

Her urgency finally seemed to register with him. 'Go where?'

'To the hospital.'

It took several seconds for her meaning to sink in; when it did he froze. 'Are you saying…?'

She nodded. 'I think…actually,' she confided, 'I'm pretty sure I'm in labour. I've had this funny feeling all day and a backache and just now I…' She took a deep breath. 'Yes, I'm definitely in labour.'

'You're going to have the baby?' Despite his flat level tone there was an undercurrent of panic in his voice that irrationally made Megan feel much calmer.

'Well not here and now…I hope.' The last vestige of colour fled his face and Megan added hastily. 'Only joking.'

'Don't,' he pleaded with feeling.

'I think a sense of humour is going to be essential.'

'Let me think,' Luc said, pressing his hands to his head as if to speed up the process. 'I'll call an ambulance. Don't worry, everything's going to be fine.'

'Or you could drive me…?' she inserted gently.

pered in his ear. 'It's going to take a lot more than a moment or even two.'

'Sounds good to me,' Luc murmured, as, hand in hand, they went to attend to the demands of their new daughter.

MILLS & BOON

**Volume 8
on sale from
6th February
2005**

Lynne
GRAHAM

International Playboys

*The Unfaithful
Wife*

4 FREE

BOOKS AND A SURPRISE GIFT!

We would like to take this opportunity to thank you for reading this Mills & Boon® book by offering you the chance to take FOUR more specially selected titles from the Modern Romance™ series absolutely FREE! We're also making this offer to introduce you to the benefits of the Reader Service™—

- ★ FREE home delivery
- ★ FREE gifts and competitions
- ★ FREE monthly Newsletter
- ★ Exclusive Reader Service offers
- ★ Books available before they're in the shops

Accepting these FREE books and gift places you under no obligation to buy, you may cancel at any time, even after receiving your free shipment. Simply complete your details below and return the entire page to the address below. You don't even need a stamp!

YES! Please send me 4 free Modern Romance books and a surprise gift. I understand that unless you hear from me, I will receive 6 superb new titles every month for just £2.69 each, postage and packing free. I am under no obligation to purchase any books and may cancel my subscription at any time. The free books and gift will be mine to keep in any case.

P5ZED

Ms/Mrs/Miss/Mr ....Initials ....

BLOCK CAPITALS PLEASE

Surname ....

Address ....

....

....Postcode.......................

Send this whole page to:
UK: FREEPOST CN81, Croydon, CR9 3WZ